The Sabbatical

Frederick Pinto

ISBN: 1-4750-0426-5
ISBN-13: 978-1-4750-0426-7

PUBLISHED AUGUST 1ST, 2012

If, once upon a time, we publicly pretended to believe, while privately we were skeptics or even engaged in obscene mocking of our public beliefs, today we publicly tend to profess our skeptical, hedonistic, relaxed attitude, while privately we remain haunted by beliefs and severe prohibitions.

– Slavoj Žižek, God in Pain

When everything is coming your way, you're in the wrong lane.

– Steven Wright

Chapter 1

"Well, not *fired*, Charles," Colin says. "Consider it more a forced buy-out."

He avoids my eyes, tapping his fingers against his pant leg. The words are clear, but their meaning is trickling in at a much slower pace. Mind kicks in, seeking perfect retort. Something cutting, clear. Words to defeat, disembowel, unmask, expose the emperor. Hell, post pictures of the naked bastard all over the Internet. Cinematic fucking grace. Instead, a heavy, paralyzing silence takes grip of me.

"They say it's definitive," he continues. "But look at the bright side. Your rep is still golden. And your package is absolute first class."

"Package?" I eke out, relieved to discover my voice still exists.

"Yes, your severance," he looks away briskly. "Everything's on the high-end. Way beyond the buy-out provisions in your contract. We want to make this as smooth as possible, Charles, and...."

"So you're telling me you're in with these guys?" I belt out. "And you really think any of this is going to go *smoothly*?"

"Yes," he snaps back. "Look, we...." He hesitates and shuffles the thick stack of documents in front of him. "*They* respect how far you've taken the company. And they know you're not one to back down from anything. But they've turned every stone on this. You'll realize it when you have time to process things. There's nothing to be gained on either side if this turns into a protracted fight."

I picture him rehearsing this two dollars' worth of horseshit in front of a mirror.

"So what are you – *they* – what are *they* proposing exactly, Colin?"

"Simple," he says. "In return for the more than generous buy-out sum, you leave the digital entertainment and music industries for two years instead of one. No lawyers, no media, no drama. Non-disclosures on everything. It's the Mind Ventures way."

He slides the documents toward me.

"The details are in here. And it all needs to happen within the next two weeks, at the latest. Things will only get worse for you after that."

"Colin," I say, struggling to stay composed, blood rushing to my extremities, "work with me here. Not an hour ago, the head of business at Sony was pitching me on a North American first dibs deal. Which I was in the process of rejecting, mind you, because *I*," I pause and lock in on his eyes, "*I*, the fucking *founder* of this damn company, am in charge of

PlayLouder's strategic vision. I just signed sixty-three goddamn checks for this week's payroll! And I'm supposed to accept this like I'm reading the morning paper?"

He looks away.

"Are they even coming in here to explain what the fuck is going on?" I yell out. He takes a small step back, afraid, it seems, that I might lunge toward him.

"They said there's not much left to talk about," he says, more subdued this time. "Traffic has slowed down since the acquisition, and revenues haven't scaled the way they'd projected. And also, most of your hard functions are either outsourced now or can be replaced."

"*Replaced*?" I ask. "By who?"

He's playing with his pen nervously. "Well, the music preference projector software I'd developed ... the one you never wanted to use. I just finished a new version of it, and it now...."

I squeeze out a weird laugh and he takes another half-step back.

"This isn't a one man show anymore," he continues, voice getting smaller. "They said they couldn't justify it being run like one."

Colin was my first recruit at PlayLouder – my own freshly graduated software geek. While I scoured the clubs and venues, converting artists to the gospel of my new project one at a time, he was turning my mad ideas into executable code. He was also good with all the things I'd never tamed: numbers, papers, filings, forms – the endless and faceless insanity of what they call *administration*. Through the years, he'd become the perfect office manager as petty chief – in control of all the life-draining details, velvety to those above him, nagging and disciplinarian to those below. And yet, I'd always somehow taken his frigid disposition as a brand of loyalty; convinced myself that his inability for even the most basic human warmth was just a function of his focus on the task at hand. But staring at him now, straight, paralyzed lips, two lifeless blue pellets for eyes, an image made up of hundreds of smaller Colin moments emerges before me for the first time. That of a silent robot who'd slowly turned my breathing animal into a lifeless machine. The hand behind the bizarre estrangement that had been creeping up on me during the last few months, like a deadly virus with only the most benign of initial symptoms. The kind of enemy clever enough to always keep invisible.

"Colin," I say, working to keep my voice flat. "This is fucking bullshit, and you know it."

"I'm sorry." He slides the file marked "CHARLES BARCA SEVERANCE" toward me.

I snatch it and walk out.

"Mr. Barca!" Average number 7 jumps in front of me enthusiastically. "I need ten for the Metric show tonight!"

The usual pre-weekend bustle emanates from the workstations of the programmers and online marketers. Office hours at PlayLouder run from 11 a.m. to 10 p.m., and the marketers are fully expected to pack on another half-day of event-hopping after that. Not that they mind; much the opposite. In fact, the night-life goodies are the reason we get away with paying them as little as we do. An addiction to music is job requirement number one, and we've got all of them. From witty hipsters to trendy club-goers, all the way through the urban hip hoppers, Goth rockers, metalheads, ragamuffins, and early morning ravers. And then, there are the "Averages." Hired for the sole reason that our screening tests have demonstrated them to react consistently like, well, the statistical average music consumer does. These oracles of normality help us determine the precise moment when a niche phenomenon is starting to crest into the mainstream, that dull, mechanical iron lung known as pop culture. At which time we know that: (a) the scene in question is nearing the end of its artistic evolutionary path, as its leading producers will imminently start cutting and pasting the successful formulas of the past; and (b) we must invest in it heavily. In fact, the Averages may have become the most critical cog in the whole machine, even though they don't know we secretly label them that. To them, they're just like the others, working for the hot web music start-up of the day, apostles of the sacred process of picking out which artists are ripe for sale. They are, in sum, "just normal averages," and proud of it, living to the pulse of a collective ethos, instinctively connected to a kind of zeitgeist of collective banality. I've always secretly admired them for their effortless understanding of the herd's sensibilities, a quality I've never harnessed myself in light of my obsessive fascination for that overrated thing called *uniqueness*. Ultimately, what matters is that they're junkies like the rest of us, and PlayLouder's easily the best high-end pusher in town. With us, short-notice SIP (*Somewhat* Important Person) access to any live music show in the Western world is all but assured.

"Mr. Barca?" Average 7 repeats, when I don't answer him the first time. "I know it's a bit unusual, but I was told by Jen to come see you directly and you would probably okay it, because...."

"Not now." I rush past him.

Heads rise above cubicle partitions in my direction. I duck into my office, making sure I close the door quietly behind me rather than slam it. I sit down, mind blank, take a quick, panoramic look around. Six years. I fumble for the phone to call Andy, my personal lawyer, but quickly hang up as I figure the bastards must have me on tap. I toss some personal items on a chair in front of me: a black 2012 agenda with only a few scribbled notes in it, three books (*Online Venture Management*, *Getting to Yes*, *Lolita*), a never used Mont Blanc pen. I take a glance outside my window. The Mount Royal, in its grand, Hollywood Hills-wannabe glory, rusty white retro metallic cross mimicking the epic HOLLYWOOD inscription. My daily reminder, over the last six years, of how – despite one's best efforts at evolution – life in Montreal is eternally governed by the forces of the irrational. My office door opens swiftly, as only one person would dare to.

"Line two," my personal assistant Clarice says, leaning on the door jamb. "They say it's important."

"E-mail the message to me," I say. "Personal e-mail please. Need to rush out for an emergency." I do my best to sound normal – casual with a trace of indifference.

"Well, *okay*," she quips, in that smart-ass tone I've come to read as, "It's your company, you can fuck it up if you want."

I feign a smile, take my bag and walk out of the office slowly, projecting my patented brand of victorious confidence as best I can. She doesn't know it yet, no one in here does. But somehow, I do. I will never be back.

Chapter 2

"It's more complicated than that," I holler over the music.

"I don't get it, then!" He answers, his well-meaning intentions veering into desperation. "It's *your* fucking company!"

David's an almost genetic carbon copy of me: part wasp, part wop, all ambition, personality sprinkled with vague remnants of family guilt, identity splintered by a thorough rejection of traditional values, built back up via post-industrial hyper modernism, big chip on his shoulder since birth. The only difference is my one quarter Jewish, which has only served to amplify all of the above to the tune of an unshakable paranoia.

I look around, mind buzzing hard. I feel like living death, but at least I'm in the right place for the occasion. Ostrich heads hanging loose, Czech language engravings lining the walls, darkness pushing against the faint candle light, steady flows of piss-warm beer muffling the wicked laughter of shady characters. Bily Kun is the last kind of place I still enjoy in this city: the kind that makes me feel I'm *not* in this city. The absinthe is cutting through my system quickly, and not the herb-infused substitute sold in the mainstream bars of Saint Laurent Boulevard. The original Czech version. The one that makes cutting one's ear off seem like a plausible response to life's inescapable quandaries.

I'm on my third, and the wormwood is meshing with the blaring sounds, drowning my thoughts in a green swivel, round and round. I'd gladly take any other drug I could grab hold of at the moment, but David insists that I ingest dose after dose of the most terrifying one of all: reality.

"Alright," I say, struggling to keep focus, "the venture cap guys, from last year, right?" He nods. "Well, they had this super high-priced buy-out clause in their investment contract. They said they wanted it there to protect themselves for if I went off the deep end or wacko or something. And they exercised it today. No warnings, nothing. That's pretty much it. I'm out, I know it."

"Wa.... that's fucked, man," he says, nodding solemnly, trying to console. "But, I mean, you're the modern equivalent of a business genius, Charles. There's got to be a way you can fight this. And even if you can't, it's only a job ..."

"Not a job, Dave. A self-made passion I believed in and created with my own sweat and ..."

The walls behind him are dancing to the slow blues riffs that are shooting out of the speakers. Barely ten minutes in and I'm already sick of the chit chat. Hendrix's "Red House" is blaring, the lulling electric vibrations penetrating me like a lumbar puncture through the spine. David's holding up, good sport he is. But the absinthe's in full swing, mind downshifting every few seconds, muscular system – which I now realize includes my tongue – completely gridlocked.

I get tapped on the shoulder and turn around, visuals catching up half a beat later.

"Mr. Barca! How's it going?"

A little spitfire of a thing with gleaming, dark skin. I stare at her and wait, consciously allowing awkwardness to seep in.

"South by Southwest?" she continues, undeterred. "We, um.... Wow, you really don't remember."

Some battles are lost before they even start, I want to tell her. But nothing actually comes out of my mouth.

"You took my demo over breakfast and said you'd listen and help me shop it when you got back to Montreal?"

Breakfast?

She shakes her head. "Never mind. Sorry to bother."

"You're not...." I manage, "just," I push the words out, "having," one at a time, "a shit day". Wow, I'm thinking. Harder than expected and could've gone a lot worse, all at once.

"Yeah!" She nods, grabs my hand, and lights up an earnest smile. "I know the feeling!"

Something tells me she doesn't quite.

David pours another shot. "And one for the lady!"

"Bottoms up!" she says.

Gulp, deep breath. "Your demo's still on my desk!" I belt out, way too loud, even for the bar. "I'll get to it next time I'm in the office."

Not a lie.

"Thanks! 'preciate it!" She answers, touching my forearm softly. "You know, everyone in this business likes to pretend that they support the artists, but I think you guys are the only ones who really...."

The sounds coming from her muffle up as I sink into thought. Over time, a capitalist society is doomed to become a collection of the professionally deformed, and I'm no exception. My own useful trick involves creating the illusion of hope in the minds of talented, yet struggling artists. Years of practice have helped me break it down to an infallible two-step formula: (a) recognizing that our industry is composed of crass, materialistic philistines, which I then pass as the main explanation of the artist's lack of success; then (b) setting myself as the source of said success through thinly veiled insinuations. Having typically been infected by the virus of excess idealism at a young age, most artists also need a valid reason to "sell out." So I also specialize in formulating personalized variations of such reasons all the way up the ladder of economic redemption: "Make a living doing what you love," becomes, "In life, everyone makes compromises," seamlessly bleeds into, "Unlike most, at least *you* got to keep *some* of your artistic integrity". Our company has even helped some – a select few, the chosen ones – attain the peak of the mountain: "Lighten up. Remember, you're living the dream. Think of the millions of good people who love the generic crap you now pass as music." Our unofficial company motto: "Be *less* evil." This line of work also demands us developing a stern indifference about the opinions our favourite artists will eventually form of us if (or rather, *when*) we don't help them make it big *enough*. The creative engine runs on the fuel of eternal suffering, creating an insatiable demand for new bad guys – we've had to get comfortable playing that role, on occasion. But this unfortunate downside is eventually atoned by the benefits of meeting new, wide-eyed artists with dreams of fame and fortune. Lather, rinse, and repeat. Her eyes spill into mine as she conjures up the image of a saviour. No wonder the whole dance has become so addictive.

Phone vibrates. "Sorry," I tell her.

"Hey, hey, where are you, Mister big-shot-fucking Barca?" Mandy yells out of the phone speaker.

"At Bily Kun. With David." Managing. Just, just managing.

"OK. When are you getting here?"

"What? Where?"

Guilty silence.

"You have *got* to be kidding me," she says, through a noisy background of her own.

More guilty silence.

"How about the club opening I've been telling you about for the last two fucking weeks?" she waits. "My last unofficial pre-launch?" More wait. "For my fucking show?"

"It's, uh, not ... a good time, Mandy." Weak as hell, I know it.

"What do you mean, *not a good time*?"

"I lost the company today."

We both pause for a few seconds. David's chatting with the girl and they're raising shot glasses to triumphant smiles in my direction. An overwhelming sense of dread takes grip of me. "I'll explain later, okay?" I say, finally.

"No, not okay." She hangs up.

Chapter 3

Mandy walks in, throws her purse on the sofa, walks to the kitchen without saying a word. It's pushing four a.m. I've been part of the living dead for going on twelve hours now, but my racing mind won't allow me to pass out. Any halfway decent God involved in human affairs, I keep thinking, would've at least allowed me a short nap before this shit.

Limbs splattered over the leather sectional. My sixty-inch LCD is furiously churning out ESPN reruns, over and over again, the same five fucking sports highlights, over and over and over, volume off. Remote limp in one hand, empty glass limp in the other.

She pushes past me.

Five years together and she still stuns me. Always more Victoria Secret model than genuine upstart artist. Good for me, though. We all make compromises with the baser instincts, don't we? At least mine will have been done in the name of beauty. She's wearing tight mini-shorts over slutty fishnet stockings. And over the stockings, the stomping boots. Which she promptly uses to kick my feet off the coffee table.

"Such a fucking loser," she looks down at me, lights a smoke and blows the first puff in my direction. The truth doesn't hurt nearly as much as you'd expect it to, sometimes.

"You know how important that was to me," she says. "This is *my* weekend, and you can't get outside your own fucking bloated head for one fucking night."

She looks away, waiting for an apology to reject; I offer none.

"The investors...." I say, slowly re-assembling things. "They fired ... well, bought...." I pause, as she gives me no energy to build on, then start again. "They got rid of me. I lost it. I'm out."

"I don't get it. All those fucking *sacrifices* we made! Weren't these guys supposed to take us into the *big time*?" she asks, barely concealing her sarcasm.

"Well I guess that didn't really pan out, did it?"

"Look," she says, shaking her head, landing flush back in her world, eyes on her phone as she types an SMS, "I don't really know what's going on in that life of yours, right? But you know what this weekend means to me. *Everyone*'s talking about it." Her eyes are still and calm now, as though she's watching her thoughts in live time. She gets an SMS back, and starts heading for the door.

"Some super important people were really confused that you weren't there tonight," she says. "I mean, it doesn't make sense. And I have to deal with this stuff, like, the day before the show." Her voice is just above a whisper now. For an instant, she looks soft, vulnerable, open. I feel silently closer to her than I have in months.

She puts her jacket on.

"Are you going somewhere?" I ask.

"Not good energy, Charles. Sorry. R*eally* not feeling this. I'm sleeping at Sandra's tonight. I need to be sharp for tomorrow."

She shuts the door behind her, not turning back.

Chapter 4

It all really started with the feature in *Wired.*

Six months out of my MBA at NYU, and I was still shunning the kind of six-figure status job most of my classmates had already eagerly fetched. Instead, my return to Montreal saw me hitch a Plateau apartment and indulge in the cheaply-priced hedonism I considered to be the city's only real competitive advantage over its more dynamic Anglo-Saxon counterparts. By day, I'd put my hands on any new venture that combined my two passions: music and technology. Internet radio stations, mobile music applications, content driven social networking ventures. I'd developed a firm belief in our inevitable future: freely available distractions where modern man can temporarily escape his pathetic and ever-declining existential status.

One day, I realized that one of my projects had somehow managed to hold its head above the ebbs and flows of the typically pathetic Montreal start-up life cycle. PlayLouder – aimed at creating the perfect system for locating unsigned musical talent. With a free PlayLouder account you could browse, compare, and even sign the top available talent by musical genre as easily as buying a pair of sunglasses on eBay. We'd transformed the vaunted art of talent scouting into a soon-to-be patented five-click process. A few brokered deals had kept it afloat on advance money alone, and my night escapades were helping me confirm that the project was slowly gaining unexpected credibility with some of the city's burgeoning indie scenes.

Then, *Wired*'s top honcho Chris Anderson famously placed us number three on his list of music companies that "got it," although "it" obviously meant something other than profitability. This immediately unleashed a tsunami of web traffic on us. We found out, to our dismay, that web popularity meant more *potential* revenues, and more *actual* costs, all at once. Meanwhile, labels had all but stopped giving advances altogether. Real money was harder than ever to come by. Just as we became hot stock, imminent collapse reared its mug. We could handle a couple more months of legitimate business, if that. Unless something gave, we were headed straight to the digital dumps – personal data selling, affiliate advertising, deep linking, banner ad aggregation – the real scum of the cyber-earth.

But as the company sank, I quickly rose. Swanky record launches, major label showcases. After parties and hotel lobbies. Label executives privately praised me for allowing them to finally fire their entire Artist and Repertoire departments. I got offered memberships in all the clubs that, just a couple of months earlier, would cringe at having an industry outsider like me as a member. Artists flocked to me as the new genie to rub with their wishes of riches and fame.

Meanwhile, the gluttonous hype machine marched triumphantly on, turning PlayLouder from trendy bandwagon into an infernal locomotive. My company – like the industry as a whole – was struggling monumentally. But *I* was thriving.

Every day was a new chapter in an emerging success story of me as rock star; chasing tail and small-time fame, racking up groupie phone digits and credit card debt, industry hype and petty club privileges. In short, I was a Montreal success story.

Then, Colin received a call from a New York-based venture capital firm called Mind Ventures. Wanted to fly me in for a face-to-face to offer a full funding and partnership deal. "You're running on fumes," they'd said. "With our contacts and resources, we can start growing this thing legitimately, and really cash in long term." The most irresistible of all gifts – a Devil's buffet to a starving man.

And so, I did what any sensible person would. Rolled up my sleeves and pigged out.

Chapter 5

All is clear on a beautiful Saturday afternoon in Old Montreal. The outdoor merchants are quietly setting up on the cobblestones, their faces and hopes illuminated by the glacial glare of the northern sun. The Saint Lawrence River is blaring blue and green reflections throughout my loft as I fire up the espresso machine. The water is calm today, viscous and transparent, almost beautiful. It allows me to forget – for a fleeting instant – that, in truth, it's a cesspool of lost hope, a fatally polluted hint of how great this city *might* have been as a seaside town that never was and never will be. The storefronts are crowded with young families as well as the odd group of female college students, looking for the social fix that subtly foreshadows the rest of their lives. *A job, a family, organized leisure.* Despite the contempt they naturally stimulate in me, I truly am fascinated in observing them – those who fit so casually into the larger human ant farm. How, despite their self-proclaimed "individuality", they move as a tightly knit, almost a carefully orchestrated group, to the rhythm of a lifestyle that has been handed down to them unquestioned, like the divine tables from above. Is there a hidden wisdom behind their seemingly mindless conformity? Are they really concealing the kind of dark, depressing lives I imagine them to have? To their credit, one thing they are *not* is bitter spectators. They're busy, filled with purpose, living lives that at least look and feel like compelling versions of the real thing. Life not haunted by the infinite shadow of everything it *could* be.

I know I should get up, go for a walk, breathe in the fresh autumn air, give my damaged lungs a chance. Since the investors came in, it's been months of board (bored?) meetings and sponsored launches and re-rescheduled appointments and cocktail finger-food and compliance exercises. Months of low oxygen count.

Instead, I slowly throw together my habitual hangover breakfast – half a hash joint, shot of orange juice, short black espresso, and a saltine – and turn on my laptop. Mandy's Gmail status is on busy, which means she's there, and wants to find out who has the balls to contact her anyway.

c.barca: *WTF*
(3 minutes pass)
c.barca: *??*
wildeart99: *setting up all day*
c.barca: *how could u just leave like that?? ... did u even listen? I lost the fkn company!!!*
wildeart99: *can't talk ... just super weird all this ... try coming at 8*
c.barca: *mand are you for real? This is serious!!*
wildeart99: *I'm serious too!*

c.barca: *whtvr .. pick up, I'm calling now*
wildeart99: *NO! today no good ... just come at 8 ... please please no drama*
c.barca: *you cannot fkn be for real!*
She switches her status to offline.

I spark the roach, walk to my balcony, take in that deep breath. Who am I kidding. I'm not going anywhere today. Other than that fucking show of hers.

Chapter 6

"Mr. Charles!"

"Lionel." I nod and look away as the bartender hands me a tumbler of vodka.

I'll confess to Mandy's canvases being a fair drop above passable, but the buzz in here suggests they're timeless classics. Which they most definitely are not. She has, however, successfully recreated her natural habitat: local B-list media personalities, attractive grad students, celebrity chef catering, twice-divorced banking executives. The glue that holds it all together isn't the paintings, though. It's *her*. The style, the body. The sheer human magnetism. *She* is the show, the only work of art worthy of the title in here. Everyone just angling to get their piece of the Mandy pie. Spotting her from afar, it's easy to see why: hair pulled back tightly, jungle green designer dress open to the sternum, multicolour surfer-style ruby necklace splashing down to her navel, touchy-touchy with any and all comers. Her single greatest achievement, and not a minor one: erasing the line between art exhibition and artist exhibitionism.

"Big shake up in the company, I heard?" Lionel insists, leeching for a response. "So, is it true?" he says, giving me an insider-type look. Only Lionel's not an insider. Never been within spitting distance of anything real his whole life. He's the outsider that insiders don't mind having around at social functions, because of his firm belief that said insiders are far more important than they really are.

"Always," I say. "Good times." I gulp the shot, motion for another, grab the refill and move away. He was in the middle of some sort of response, I think. He could go fuck himself.

The plan couldn't be clearer: tread water, stay light, no talk about anything remotely related to music or business or the Internet or life on planet Earth. The stares are digging in from all angles. Everyone in here either knows me or knows *of* me; I'm not sure which is worse at this point. Only now do I realize how ridiculous I must look for the occasion. Unshaven, un-showered, stoned all the way to sober, wearing my best American Apparel hoodie and dark grey jeans. Fuck them all, though, down to the last bloodsucker. Fuck them in their brains. Not worrying about the stupid dress code could be one unexpected advantage to becoming a ghost.

I squeeze past a couple of groups to finally catch sight of Mandy. She's in the zone, surrounded by two "adorable loser" hipster types, and an official-looking man in his fifties with an impeccable navy blue suit and an open white shirt. The hipsters both have thick black rimmed glasses, as well as clothes that don't match, on purpose, of course.

I find myself without the mild amusement their type normally procures me. They just induce in me a vague sense of sickness now. That whole fashion of un-fashion thing; the unbearable heaviness of fake. Their irony doesn't conceal a razor sharp intellect. It's just an empty fetish of it, another vapid symbol in a society whose soul has become spectacle.

I circle the group discreetly. I can tell Mandy is trying hard to ignore me. Everyone's blowing about some band from Brooklyn that Pitchfork has been pimping for the last few weeks. I lean in for a quick kiss, only to get cheek and a cool glare instead. She grabs my hand, squeezes hard.

"Everyone, I think you know Charles," she says, beaming. They all nod. Never seen any of them in my life.

"So, what do you think of the Brooklyn music scene of late?" hipster one asks. I look up and am surprised to see he's staring at me, waiting for a response.

"Gutless crap," I blurt out. "Castrated rock n' roll by a bunch of silver-spoon-fed art fags." I glance around and mutter to myself. "They'd probably love it here."

Silence. Uncomfortable laughter slowly spreads around.

"Ha, you almost had me there!" he says, smiling brightly. "Pitchfork says...."

"Are you fucking joking?" I say, too loudly. "Pitchfork is for hipster trash who want names of obscure bands they've never heard to name-drop at pseudo-intellectual art-house cocktail parties. Fuck Pitchfork."

Mandy's eyes inject a dose of death into my soul, while the two guys and the older man start talking to themselves lowly, pretending nothing has happened.

"If you came here to embarrass me, maybe you can just get the fuck out right now," she whispers into my skull, teeth clenched.

"Yeah, maybe I *should* leave you alone," I say. "And then you can come back home on your fucking glory fix and you can pretend to actually care that I've just lost my fucking...."

I stop as I notice her eyes welling with emotion. The crowd around us is buzzing like a colony of hungry bees. I spot a few local celebrities. This *is* the big deal she's made it out to be, I'm thinking. I feel some pride that, despite everything that's happened to me, I can manage to eke out a bit of sympathy for her.

"Hey look, it's your best friend, Anne-Marie Losique, isn't it?" I ask, meaning to relieve tension. "Don't think I've seen her since the when-she-was-fucking-Ben-Affleck days. Why does she look like a silicone-stuffed bimbo all of a sudden?" I stop and collect myself. She looks at me with, eyes gaping. "I mean ... have you asked her?" I sputter out.

She nods a slow no. "What happened to you?" she asks me, as a sharply dressed television couple swoops in behind toothy smiles, caressing her shoulder, showering us with empty compliments my ears don't register.

"I...." I hesitate, as Mandy gently caresses the couple and takes a few steps away from me.

"I'm gonna go," she says, waving at me with a blank stare as she turns into the crowd and disappears into the surrounding noise.

Woke up alone, head throbbing. Hash, OJ, syrupy coffee. Triple dose of multivitamins for health. Computer screen glare, good morning sunshine. Bookmarks, favourite blog tabs, news alerts and notices. SMS light blowing up, twenty one un-read e-mails from last night alone. My virtual self has never been more alive. News today is Facebook's top entertainment application was found to have been secretly transmitting personal user data to marketing companies. For some reason, the obvious still passes as news. Zuckerberg was the one entrepreneur always ahead of me on the cynicism curve, and he got handsomely rewarded for it. I got the voyeurism part, but never imagined that everyday folk would stoop to the same vain exhibitionism as our celebrities. The alliance between the nosey and the narcissistic – a match made in digital heaven. I realize that my own profile, with that indecent number of friends, groups and followers, probably makes it open season on whatever it is that passes as my private life. It's a strange feeling, witnessing so much activity *about* me while simultaneously feeling barely alive. The show would probably continue to go on even if I suddenly dropped dead, at least for a little while. I feel eternal for about two seconds as I realize my online identity has outgrown my physical self in relevance. I may not know who I am right now, but at least everyone else does.

Mandy has a few dozen pictures of last night up already. I'm on one of them, just before the Pitchfork moment. I can tell she was secretly praying to the gods of social etiquette that I would keep it shut for once. She was right to. But I guess they were deaf to her prayers. Maybe they hate Pitchfork as much as I do.

Her news feed: *Thx so much for the massive encouragement everyone! Big cheers to all of you for a great year! So much more to come!! Baci, xxx.*

Browsing around her profile, I also notice that she has updated her relationship status to *Single*.

I immediately call her. No answer.

A cold shower of distressed nerve-endings overtakes me. I call a second time, leaving a voicemail, "Mandy, I'm serious, please call me back *now*."

I scour through PlayLouder's Facebook profile, then website. All references to me have been deleted.

I inhale repeatedly but no oxygen seems to enter my lungs.

I go from blank mind to acute self-awareness, then back again, back and forth. But things are perfectly clear. The disintegration of my life is now a public event.

Chapter 7

"I don't understand, sir." The woman at the Delta ticket counter seems frustrated by my request. "Where to, exactly?"

"I told you, first plane to any one of these three destinations," I say for the third time, slowly enunciating each syllable. "Boston, Chicago, New York." I put the cities in alphabetical order this time, hoping that might help.

"I heard you the first couple of times," she replies curtly. "But on my screen, I need to pick an actual destination."

"And I told you. Whichever plane leaves first to one of these three places."

"Doesn't matter which?"

"Not in the least."

"Okay." She taps a few keys angrily and sighs. "Flight 1127 departs to Toronto in less than an hour. You'll have a forty-five minute layover, then connect to flight 235 going to Chicago."

"Great." I put my credit card on the counter and turn away.

Pierre Elliott Trudeau Airport is bustling with people animated by plans, purpose, schedules, duties, relationships. People moving fast in straight lines. All of it weighing down me, weighing down on life terribly.

"Return date?" she snaps.

"Umm.... No."

"So, a one-way ticket, then?"

Nothing escapes her razor sharpness. I nod, and she squeezes out a tight smile under a ruthless stare, types some more.

"See, that wasn't so hard," I say.

Giving me as close to an annoyed glare as the customer service handbook might allow, she takes my credit card and swipes it.

"Any luggage to check in today?" she asks.

"Nope," I tap my backpack. "Got everything I need, right here." I force out an uneasy smile.

She nods as though she might have something to add, but keeps it to herself.

"Passport?"

I fumble around in my pocket and, along with the passport, pull out a guest invite for an Arcade Fire launch I was invited to weeks earlier.

"Actually miss, can we change that to New York?"

She doesn't answer, pummels her keyboard, snags the credit card, swipe, sigh, tap tap tap. I feel contempt for her, then pity, then something approaching a Zen-like indifference.

"Thank you, sir. Have a great life."

Did she actually say that?

A ghost, on vodka, in the sky.

I smooth-talk the stewardess into granting me exception after exception to the three mini-bottles per passenger rule. My God-given charms will not have been granted in vain.

By the time I reach JFK, only the sunglasses save my face, and just barely. I catch a reflection of myself on a signpost. I look like Robert Downey Jr. when he looked like a drunken shit. Zigzagging toward the baggage claim area, the purpose people react to me in three synchronized steps, as though part of a socially rehearsed script: 1. indiscrete look when noticing *something* out of the ordinary; 2. mouth wide open, television stare; and 3. quick look away if and when I make eye contact. I'd fight them all off – the little demons – one by one, if I could find the strength. Instead, I fumble for my iPhone, that last remaining anchor to my life, and search for numbers starting with 212, 917, and 315, finding far fewer than I expected. Back in my NYU days, I was convinced I'd made enough friends to last a lifetime, but can barely find anyone I feel comfortable enough to reach out to now. Since college, my trips to the Big Apple have been about taming a different kind of animal – the music entrepreneur. Label people big and small, producers, managers, venue and club owners, pimps and prostitutes of all denominations in this racket of a business. A mixed bag of bandits and old foxes, peppered in by the odd, genuine success story.

I send a text to one of those, Ken Brand, my favourite up and coming hip hop mogul. No immediate answer. I reach back to the mental rolodex and try hard to think of someone with a more personal connection, and Hal's name comes up. All but written off since a night of partying had revealed he became an obnoxious, name-dropping Wall Street Lieutenant, monkey print t-shirts and world history conversations replaced by four hundred dollar jeans, shiny leather shoes and angry tirades against any idea not propelled by a Greckonian appeal to greed. One of the oft-overlooked tragedies of the hedge-fund boom: taking people who were genuine products of the 90's and teleporting them right back into the 80's. The one thing that had kept us in touch through the years was Hal's keen interest in modern art, and Mandy's constant harpings about keeping him and his contacts close to us. "I'm not asking you to *hang out* with them, Charles," she had said countless times, "but make an effort for me. They're my target market. Frustrated alpha's with *lots* of money."

Hal calls back within seconds of having received my text message.

"Hey Charlie!" he laughs out, as though in the middle of a terrific inside joke. "Long time, buddy!"

"Hey, what's up Hal," I answer, trying to hide my disappointment at actually having reached him.

"Wait, it's too early for drunk dialling. So ..." a cautious tone creeps into his voice, "who died?"

"Funny. No one." I say laconically as I stumble out of the airport. "Just in town for a couple of days. How are things?"

"Actually, amaaaazing! Business great. Just got engaged to Mel, so that's great. Reaaalllly no complaints. So, you down here partying like only the Barca train knows how?"

Barca train?

"Umm ... not sure," I say, trying to clear my brain by rubbing my suddenly glare-sensitive eyes. "There's maybe a launch thing tonight.... "

"Dude, you will *not* believe this, but this is actually crazy timing!" He brings his voice down to a hoarse whisper. "Mel's out of town on business! Let's do this! Parties are all that's left in the music biz, right! I mean, that and PlayLouder, right?"

"Yeah, about that...."

"Look, can't chat now, darting into a meeting for the afternoon. My place at eight-ish and we take it from there?"

"I guess, but I ..." I start, mind unable to generate an excuse on time. "Sure," I relent.

"Nice! I'm texting you the address now. I'll take care of the goodies. See you later!"

He hangs up the phone before I can reply.

Barely a minute later, Ken Brand sends me an SMS: *Got ur message, in meetings ... have a soft launch party tonight – can u join? big things to discuss ... can have u picked up anywhere anytime ... let me know. K.*

I scour New York's streets, as opposed to its boardrooms, for the first time in years. The big city pace is already slowing things down in my head. I still have distant images of Gotham back when it was all guts and grit, back before tough guy Rudy exported the testosterone to the peripheries and ushered in the era of nanny-state castrations and rampant metro-sexuality. Grabbing my espresso from a busy barista for whom my existence seems like a minor annoyance, watching the iPod drones hover glass-eyed around me, caught up in the utmost *rational organization of life*, I just can't imagine things combusting into the kind of spontaneous adventure mode I'm craving. The real price of the society of unlimited access: losing the amazement that only comes with the struggle against limitations. The sense of journey, snuffed out by an eternal present of moving frames.

I pace the pavement with increasing speed. A ghost feels best when it's anonymous, burying itself deep within the busy vibrations of the herd. Strangers indifferently brush past me, and it feels great. Those who don't care have one great thing in common with those who care the most: they've lost the faculty to judge you. *Sometimes you want to go ... where nobody knows your name*. My iPhone's been whining non-stop and I've been ignoring her, until I finally relent and notice about a dozen unread items. The last one catches my attention. It's from Clarice, with no subject, which she knows is the likeliest way to get me to read it.

> *Charles, I'm writing from my personal e-mail – please reply here, I don't want to get in trouble ... where are you? Everyone's going crazy here. Word is you're on leave ... is that true? Colin's very distant. The lawyers were here for*

a full day yesterday. What's going on? I'm on your side ... Waiting for your reply soon. Clarice.

I write back: *I'll let you know when I can think of one.*

"And this one right here," Hal yells out, as he points to an undecipherable mess of a dismembered animal painting on his wall. He snorts another line and shoves the silver tray toward me. "Got it for thirty K eleven months ago. Now worth?"

"I don't know," I sigh and put the tray down next to my lap. "Tell me, Hal."

"C'mon, just guess!"

"Ten million."

"A hundred and fifty K! And they're waxing about a bust real estate bubble! The talking-heads on CNN Money should've told the middle class about Christie's-sponsored, Somali-born abstract impressionists instead, don't you think? Hahahaha! Fuck Fanny *and* Freddie! Whup whup!"

We're having to scream just to hear each other against the loud hip hop booming out of his designer speakers (... *I just wanna fuck every girl in the world* ...). Back at NYU, Hal would've easily been voted most likely to spend the rest of his days wearing sandals – hair perpetually messy, beard untrimmed, always waxing proudly about travel adventures in remote places. Now, he looks perfectly good-man: gelled brown hair, fashionable stubble and benevolent eyes – a face tailor made for life-insurance and lifestyle drug peddlers. That, along with his over-the-top positivity, takes some edge off the verbal torrent emerging from him.

"So, you having some or what?" he bawls, pointing to the small white mound.

"I'll pass, thanks," I say and look away. He catches me glancing at his enormous TV.

"Eighty-inch HD prototype, with built in Blue-Ray burner and PVR! Wicked, no?"

"Indeed."

"Some dude at work just sent me ALL of Entourage Season Eight! It's not even out yet! Wanna watch some?"

"Not now, it's cool."

"Charles, *come on*!" he shoves the coke-filled tray back toward me, spilling enough on me to feed his artist's Somali village for a month. "For old time's sake, let's go!" he insists.

I relent and snort one line to his three, even though we've never, to my recollection, done anything like this in the past. His phone rings.

"Oh fuck.... Sshhhh! Quiet down for a sec. It's Mel. Wait." He hushes loudly, rubbing his nose and clicks the mute button of his system, sending one final echo shooting through the penthouse as it goes instantly silent.

"Hey, babe! Yeah ... yeah, okay, I'll pick'em up ... okay ... yeah. Guess who's here? Charles Barca! Yeah, with me, right now! What time you getting back tomorrow? Great. See you for dinner? I told you, I'll ... look, I'll call you back a bit later, okay? Charles is waiting for me. Okay. Love you too!"

He hangs up, and the beats go blaring again.

"It's never enough attention for them, you know? Speaking of, how's Mandy? I heard she blew up the fucking block at her show! Three Merryl VP's and my boss Steve Waymire were there! And these guys are like the real authentic shit. HUGE spenders. And they've been talking Mandy up like crazy...."

"Yeah, don't know. Look, why don't we get out of here?"

"Now you're talking, Barca! So, and please don't shit you me," he suddenly stops moving and stares me down, "are we really meeting Ken Brand tonight? 'Cause I already told a couple of guys at work and they don't...."

"Maybe. But I have to hit this Arcade Fire thing first."

"Oh, right. You and that hipster thing again." He snorts another. "You guys in Montreal are all love that crap. Figures. Your city's the only place the Anglo male's a persecuted minority in pretty much all the English-speaking world. That's where he learned to become a self-deprecating loser version of himself."

"Hal?"

"Yes?"

"Please don't be an ass, okay?"

"Me? An ass?" he asks, winking through a huge smile, and we walk out.

"Fuckin' Converse Chuck Taylors an' fag 'staches," Hal grumbles through his teeth, under his breath and into my ears, as we walk into the Mercury Lounge, "an' fake ass sailor bullshit virility act, and...."

"Hey!" I grab his shoulders and stop him; his lost, wild stare makes me look away and just drag him along.

He follows, quietly eyeing around in acrimony now, as I spot Shelley Weinberg, my ticket into this place. Her unassuming thrift wear and humble smile belies the fact that she's the top indie talent manager in the city. I feel good seeing someone from a scene that actually supported me during my beginnings in this business, like I'm rejoining a home crowd that appreciates me. Or at least should, I'm thinking. I motion Hal to settle down one more time before I walk up to her.

"Charles!" she reaches out warmly and kisses me on the cheek. "You never confirmed you'd be showing! You look good!"

"Thanks," I answer. "Been working out."

She laughs, apparently getting a sarcasm I employed only half-consciously.

"This is Hal," I say. "A friend from way back."

He nods, and quickly looks away from her, scouring the scene for his idea of action. She flashes a quick frown in his direction and turns back to me.

"You *just* missed the main set," she says. "Stick around though. My next big thing's starting a longer set in a few minutes. I've been meaning to talk to you about them."

I sense Hal fidgeting and suffering silently behind us.

"They're called the Dark Knights," Shelley continues. "I wanted to maybe do a featured blast with you guys next month...."

"Shelley, I'm not...."

"Dark Knights? What, like the superhero?" Hal slobbers out through an incredulous look.

"Uhh ... yeah?" Shelley answers, annoyed.

"Ha!" he says, looking away now. "Real original. Charles, what are we drinking?"

Shelley stares at Hal with an irritated look I've never seen from her. "It's actually a critique of Bruce Wayne as the modern man," she says, angling for his attention. "You know, a lonely prisoner in a golden castle, putting a suit by day, fighting to keep an illusion of order in a hopeless urban jungle where everyone, even the government, is corrupt." Shelley speaks sharp and fast, like a quick little Wicca. "It's actually quite brilliant," she says.

"Cute," Hal says, not skipping a beat. "But you guys are still not rock and roll. Never never will be. Just a sad version of it."

I now remember that, back in school, Hal had been one of the shrewdest interpreters of pop culture I'd ever met. Which makes me realize, now, how highly conscious his current life choices must be.

"I mean, you've replaced these demi-gods," he continues, "with what? You killed the Morrisons and the Jaggers and the Plants, and gave us what exactly? *This* shit?" He points to a guy standing next to Shelley in a purple and orange striped sweater and extra tight gray jeans.

In one instant, I feel embarrassed and remember why I'd made friends with this guy, all at once.

"Batman does risk his life to fight the bad guys," I offer to Shelley, trying to lighten things. "I mean, at the end of the day, he's a good guy, right?"

"Yeah," Shelley says, staring at Hal with vitriol. "But he's not doing it to restore a healthy society, like Superman did in the Fifties. He does it because his parents got murdered when he was kid. He's self-centered and psychotic. He's got all the money in the world, but his only friends are Alfred and Robin – basically the help, right? His refuge is his Bat Cave of toys and entertainment. And even if he beats the bad guys, his life won't change. He'll still be a tormented loner. We all know a few candidates for that kind of life, don't we?" She points her eyes toward Hal slightly, which he notices.

"Great. All I need." He says, to himself, but no doubt louder than he's intending. "Another duelling dyke in my life."

"What?" Shelley says, stepping toward him. "What did you say? Charles, what did this guy just say?"

Some nearby people turn toward us. I'm surprised, as I've never seen Shelley's temperature rise above even.

"What?" Hal says, eyes shifting like a madman's, clearly beyond talk.

"Okay, enough!" I say, taking Hal to the side. "Hal, outside!"

"What? I'm cool!" he says. "It's not *my* fault she's a socially mal-adapted duelling dyke!"

"Out!" I say, pushing him away. "Let me do some damage control out here," I tell him, when we're a few steps away. "I'll call Ken. Maybe we'll go to his thing instead."

"Yeah, screw this place!" Hal says, as I make sure to escort him all the way outside. I text Ken and circle back inside to Shelley.

"Hey, I'm super sorry about that," I tell her. "I don't know what's up with him, he's just on a lot of coke and...."

"It's okay, Charles," she says. "You should know better than bringing a guy like that to a place like this."

"Agreed," I answer, and her sweet face invites me to confide. "Look, I wanted to tell you, something happened at work. I'm sort of not ... kind of not in the picture anymore."

I pause, unsure what to expect from her. She briefly frowns, thinking to herself.

"What do you mean, not in the picture?"

"Yeah, it's a crazy story. Basically I'm officially not part of PlayLouder anymore. I have some suspicions as to how it happened, but who cares, right? I'm just ... I don't know. Guess I'm trying to figure out what comes next for me, and thought maybe we could …"

"Charles," she stops me, still visibly flustered, "you think we can talk about this sometime next week? There's some people I really have to get back to. Here," she motions to the bartender, "have a drink on me, okay?"

She pulls back while squeezing my shoulder, keeping eye contact. "Seriously, I do want to know what happened. Enjoy the show for now. We'll talk later, okay?"

I'm forced to nod, and she gives me a final hand grab before walking away.

I take in a big gulp of vodka and feel absorbed by the big, scenic sounds of the wailing guitars and pouncing snares of the band. A now familiar dizziness sets on me. My eyes are half-closed and I dream up an almost visual flashback of some drifting images: my Mind Ventures agreement, my last speech at the Googleplex, Colin in his consciously understated suit – and then I get hit by thoughts of Mandy. Without thinking much, I take out my iPhone and text her: *Mandy .. what's going on*?

I sigh deeply and take in another gulp. A couple of minutes later, I receive a text. It's from Ken.

The music business is – even at its best and squeaky cleanest – sketchy business. But Ken Brand is the absolute real deal. He's the music Midas of the day, a bona fide oracle of pop. We were both speakers at MIDEM, the annual industry whore show in Cannes, and walked away with genuine appreciation for one another. He instantly became one of the most high-profile backers of PlayLouder.

"Dude, this is SO much better!" Hal says giddily, as we walk into The Box, a small venue off of Bowery. "I think I see him back there!"

We reach the back of the club and I spot Ken in a sleek, dark suit, dreadlocks hidden under a black Kangol hat, a posse of about half a dozen surrounding him. He steps toward me as soon as he sees me.

"This is Charles, everyone!" Ken proclaims. "King and castle of the online music world!"

I laugh off the attention and try in vain to get closer to him. "Actually, man...." I try, but he's already onto someone and something else.

Hal taps my shoulder, "dude, can you introduce us?" He says, as he ogles two barely legal, scantily dressed glittering girls in Ken's entourage.

Before I can answer, one of Ken's friends jumps out in front of me.

"Hey, wassup, Mr. Barca? My man Ken's said lots of amazing things about you, all you guys. You got an amazing product, but I guess you know that. Look, me and a partner are workin' hard on starting up this new label gig. Got our hands on some of Tupac's unreleased recordings. We'd love to set up something big with you guys. And it has to make sense for you too, obviously. Right now though, only thing is, Afeni's being a total snag man, she's...."

"Look man," I get closer to him and whisper, so as not to make a scene, "I can't do anything for you right now. I'm sure your project's great and all, and this would take too long for me to explain. But just trust me. I'm not who you think I am."

He takes a step back, and the excited look on his face quickly turns to ice. I gravitate back toward Ken, who waves for me to join him. I squeeze past the two girls, whom Hal is now chatting up, as one of them tries hard to make eye contact with me.

"Mr. Barca, Mr. Barca," Ken says, in a fake formal way, his classy Rasta act and firm, thoughtful mannerisms conspiring to give him a compelling magnetism. "Come and sit here. It's a most pleasing coincidence that you are here with me and my closest entourage tonight. As you know, our operation has reached a whole new maturation point. Our 360 deals have been very successful, particularly our marquee-touring arm." I listen, waiting to interject. For some reason I feel like I could confide in Ken. He's from the proverbial streets, knows at least as much as I do about the ruthless rollercoaster of success and failure in a declining industry. But he's the narrative equivalent of a freight train. His eyes swirl in menacing pools of red, his diction is perfect, his innate sense of rhythm giving him an unusual, persuasive aura. I could try to stop him, but it would be entirely at my own risk.

"Our needs have overgrown what our major label partners can now offer," he continues. "The old structures have become too expensive compared to what they provide." He pauses and stares deeply into my eyes, making sure I'm giving him my full attention. "So, here we are."

Hal jumps in next to us and says to Ken, "Hey, what's up brother? I don't say this lightly, but I'm a real fan of your work! I...."

"We are going all independent," Ken turns back to me, ignoring Hal. "We don't need anyone to bankroll our operations no more. You know what I'm talking about better than anyone, Charles. We can piecemeal better distribution and marketing than they could possibly provide. Big Brother is beat the fuck up. It's taking my team about six to twelve months to iron out the details, but it's time for us to claim the kingdom that is rightfully ours. And together with PlayLouder, we can build the perfect online showcase for all our artists. The smaller ones we will build on the back of the bigger ones, flip them for cash whenever we can. You guys provide the back-end technology, we can do the rest from our own self-marketed online window. I've got my pulse on the beat, Charles. You know it. And you know me, Chucky. I WAS BORN TO BE KING!" He suddenly breaks into a long, uncontrollable laugh and raises his cup high for all around to see. They all raise their glasses to heed the monarch's call.

I smile and follow along, then quietly pull him aside.

"Ken, there's something I've been wanting to tell you. Something big." That finally captures his attention.

"Course, speak up, brother Barca." He looks at me attentively. "I'm all ears."

"I'm ... kind of not at PlayLouder anymore. Got ambushed, man," I say with an exhalation, waiting for the visual cues prefiguring a response. I can almost sense his heart rate drop.

"Why.... What?" he asks. "Why don't I know this? When?"

"It just happened. I'm sure it'll come out in industry news soon enough. You're among the first to know on my side of things."

"Wow ... wow," he says, mind seeming to drift. "Isn't that your company though?" He stops, thinks, starts again. "And your friends – the other ones – are they still there?"

"Yeah, most of them. I think some were even in on the coup. I may fight it still. I don't know. Look, shit happens I guess, I just want to figure what I want next...."

He nods pensively, holding up two fingers to halt whatever was coming next from me.

"Wait. Band on." He gets up to rejoin a group of four at the edge of the VIP, closer to the stage.

Instead of following him, I sit and look around. Hal is on the white leather couch, suavely gesturing at the two girls. They all hold eye contact with me for a second, as though they're talking about me and want to elicit a reaction. He waves for me to join them; one of the girls smiles invitingly in approval. I know them by heart, those nightlife vamps, hunting for a pint of fame here, a pound of status there; those tweet-chique groupie types whose gibberish runs in fast forward, junkies of tweener pop stars and the Disney channel by age seven, suburban beauty pageants between nine and twelve, then drugs and uniforms and public toilet blowjobs, then college and amateur porn cams, followed by entry-level jobs and hard partying on the back of a vulgar hotness and loud make-up and sophomoric life theories, culminating into some version or other of the American way of life and a high-earning beta male they can blood suck into a castrating relationship of mortified sex and consumerism and debt and death.

Hal motions, more insistent. The girls stare on with lust. I return a school-boy smile, sit a few steps away, gather myself and start listening to the band. Really nice. Live strings and horns, top lyrical flow. Their only shortcoming – an excess of originality. They'll inevitably become someone's marketing nightmare. A few thousand dedicated fans, maybe six digit hits on their MySpace later, they'll discover that their upside is paying the bills like the rest of us. I shake my head, thinking of how – from their former status as heroes and icons – music artists have now become just another sub-species in a bland, Western middle-class jungle.

Hal appears in front of me and snaps me back into the moment. "Hey dude, you partying or what?"

"Yeah, sure," I answer as he puts a bulky bump of blow on top of my hand, which I snort without thinking. I pull back, the vodka turns into water, and our two little friends have suddenly become a lot more attractive.

"You look a bit out of it, man," Hal says. "Awesome fucking spot, though!"

"Yeah. I'm good," I say, mouth dry, mind dark and absent.

"Cool, 'cause you KNOW I'm there if there's anything, right?"

He squeezes my shoulder. I feel a pang of grief run up my sinuses, which I immediately suppress by hauling in another full mouth of Grey Goose.

"Take a picture of us!" One of the girls comes over and asks me. She hands me her iPhone and, before I can answer, she sexy mooches her friend on the cheek, the friend kissing toward the camera. I snap and hand it back to her.

"Okay, now you and me," she says to me, handing the phone to the friend.

"Wait," I say.

"Shhhhh!" she says, then wet mooches my cheek; snap, flash. Hal wrestles the phone from the friend, starts French-kissing her ear. My heart is beating fast and three demons are urging it to go faster. I turn and walk up to Ken, before things deteriorate into their inevitable, muddled mess.

"Ken, can we talk?"

"Sure, what's up," he says, eyes onstage.

"Look, I consider you a real friend. Can I level with you?"

"Of course!"

"Can we sit down sometime this week?" An adrenaline rush seeps up my spine, and I'm suddenly unsure of what will come out of my mouth next.

"This week is tough," he says, still looking away. "Real tough week."

Ken has never treated me with anything less than borderline reverence. A surge of anger rises up my neck and chest.

"But hey, I'm going to give Colin a call and check out what's going on out there," he continues, flashing that big Ken smile at me. "And if I hear anything, of course I'll let you know. You my white nigga, Barca!"

He turns, and slams his large hand against the back of my shoulder, takes a few steps into the crowd.

Returning to the table I swallow two more shots, then take another bump. Everyone disappears, and I speed walk back toward him.

"Hey, Ken!" I bark out. The drug is now swimming happily in me, the lights in the club shining as bright as a midday Caribbean sun.

"Yes?" He answers, barely turning around toward me.

"Listen!" I demand, almost screaming in his ear now. "You wanna be bleeding edge, Ken? You wanna be on top of this shit pile we somehow still call an industry? Then listen!"

His eyes fix mine firmly.

"PlayLouder is the goddamn past. They just got scared of how far I was willing to take things," I say. "These new investors come in, with their flow charts and stupid linear projections that never materialize. I was too revolutionary for them. There's a bigger – much bigger – picture out there. In six months, PlayLouder will be a joke, a relic of the past like the rest of them. And if you tie your operation down to them, you'll go right down the sinkhole, too."

I must have struck some kind of nerve, as he's listening intently now.

"You want to miss the boat?" I continue. "Then go call Colin. Join the establishment's new gadget. I'm at the point where I need to know who my troops are. I'm taking clients in at the ground level. That's why I wanted to see you."

"You speakin' truth, Barca?"

"Listen, I built that show, and I'm stronger than ever now. The pirates threw me out, but they have no clue how to run a ship like that, let alone build a newer and better one. Now I'm blowing them out and there's nothing they can do about it. Yeah, I'm for real. The real question is – are *you* for fucking real, Kenny?"

Barely having said that, I gain a new, visceral appreciation for the art of knowing when to shut up. But the rush is doing the talking for me, and Ken's surprised reactions are only fueling the unholy shipwreck.

"So that's why you in New York?" he says with a friendly grin.

"What do you think," I say, "I was looking for a fucking shrink? No disrespect, but you're not exactly Sigmund fucking Freud!"

We break into an affectionate laugh at the same time. And all it took was a little bullshit, I'm thinking. *Open sesame music industry.*

"Okay, so what exactly is this new thing of yours?" Ken asks. "And how do you see us working together?"

"Look, let's not talk details now. I just wanted to know where your head was. But you develop your showcase with PlayLouder, and we can't do this. That's my only thing. I can hit you up with everything later."

"Okay, well I'm in no rush," Ken says. "I've always been down with you, you know that. You're a pioneer and so am I. I understand sometimes you gotta kill the big brother so you can move on. Just give me a little glimpse...."

"Hey, come on, let's take it easy tonight," I say and raise my glass to Hal and the girls. "This band is great. And we'll get down to business soon enough."

My phone rings like a distant cry in a wild, dizzy jungle. Eyes crack open, walls spinning, head pounding. I peel the girl's arm off my chest just enough to get a glimpse. Hal's on the other bed, cupping with his matrimonially. Disgusted, I decide to make for a quick exit. I take my iPhone to the bathroom, throw some water on my face, and click on an e-mail from Colin titled "Immediate Action Requested":

Dear Charles:

You are obviously above returning messages. Hopefully you realize we just want to close this out asap. It is not in the interest of anyone to have this drag on, least of all you. All we need is your signature. Otherwise we will have no choice but to exercise the contractual clause, which would play against you. We need to make closing arrangements within 48 hours if you want to avoid escalation.

I crash on the sofa chair, fumble for the pack of cigarettes that's lying there. I light up, bask in the smoke for a bit. I notice a sheet hung atop the desk, reminding me that the reason the room is non-smoking is to "ensure my full comfort and enjoyment."

Hal turns on the TV, waking the girls up.

"Wow, guys. Crazy night!" he says. The girls are all whispers and giggles. I'm thankful to have next to no memory of the night's end. Then, more disgust, more smoke, zoning in on Hal's neurotic dashing through the fifty-seven channels of nothing on, before he stops on MSNBC.

"Hal, can you put the volume down?" I say. He looks at me with a surprised look.

"Someone woke up on the wrong side...."

"Please?"

He obliges.

I walk to the small desk and open my laptop, pretending everyone into disappearance.

"Hey, should we get some breakfast in here?" Hal says enthusiastically.

"Okay!" one of the girls answers. "But we have to go soon!"

I head for Facebook and quickly scan the collection of "WTFs" and "OMGs" and "IMOs" from people I barely know that now litter my wall. I click around to find out about deleting my account, then realize all those photos and comments about me will survive all the same, and I can just re-log in and reactivate the whole nightmare anytime I want, anyway. Always a step ahead, that Zuckerberg kid. Once your face is booked, you're fucked for good.

Mandy's news feed: *Love is a dog from hell.* Impressive. Probably the work of some literary type chasing tail. Whatever. I glance at the TV, and it stops me cold. My picture, to the left of the female presenter's head. It's my corporate headshot: open-collared striped shirt, hair just shy of bed-head, the confident smile. A Leibowitz, for the cover of *Fast Company.*

"Hal! Raise the volume!"

"Hey, can you make up your –"

"Now!"

"... Ousted from the company he founded. Barca was widely seen as the force that lured in the top up and coming talent to PlayLouder and, in doing so, changed the face of the industry forever. With Barca gone, insiders report that even long-term staffers are fearing the pink slips. One can only wonder if the company's rock n' roll roster won't follow in their tracks, leaving PlayLouder, our Loser of the Week."

They all turn toward me in synch.

"Dude, you didn't say...." Hal says.

"Was that you?" Hal's girl asks me, hand hiding mouth. "Oh my god!" She takes her iPhone, snaps a shot of me, starts thumbing.

"Okay girls, time to go," Hal starts walking them to the door.

"I'm listening," he says when he comes back.

And I begin.

He crosses his arms with a serious stare, seeking the right words.

"Look man, you're this outlier, this prince among men in your industry, right?"

"Yeah," I lift my eyes. "A bought-out, spit-over, disgraced and depressed prince, if that qualifies as royalty in your lexicon."

"Can I be honest?"

I nod.

"This is the best thing that could've happened to you."

I hold, gauging his look for an extra second. Despite his goofy appearance, I'd always projected onto Hal a viciously sharp intelligence, a practical brand of brains I'd only been able to apply to my own life in short, unpredictable spurts.

So I force myself to give him the benefit of at least some modicum of doubt.

"I'm listening," I say.

"You got enough money to get by?"

"More than I need."

"So fuck it. Just move on!"

"Fuck it?"

"Yes! Okay, where do I even start? Why did you go back to Montreal?"

"What, after New York? I don't know. Roots, I guess." I say, fully sensing the lameness of my answer.

He lets out a loud, mocking guffaw. "Bullshit!" he says. "You didn't go back for roots. That trip to Prague fucked you up. I don't think you remember. You came back all weirded out. I remember you saying you'd met real artists there, touring around Europe for fun with no career prospects, just living day by day, like crazy troubadours. You became obsessed with making a *difference* and revolutionizing the market for them, and all kinds of that airy-fairy, utopian stuff. You could barely hide your contempt for those of us who were looking for normal careers. In year two of an NYU MBA, Charles, for Christ's sake!" he says. "You must've noticed. Everyone in the program thought you were a freak. That's why you went back to Montreal. Because an elite level job just wasn't good enough for you. You wanted to go back home to become some sort of hero."

"Right, and look at what happened next," I retort. "I founded one of the top music companies around, made a difference in the lives of dozens of artists. Meanwhile, the rest of them – including you, I might add – got locked up in soul-destroying, high-paying slavery gigs. So, you tell me, what was I supposed to do instead? Get a job I *didn't* love just so I could feel better when I lost it?"

"Well, you probably loved your project when it started. But then you decided to bring professional investors in. Look, I'm not even sure what happened there exactly, but with that personality of yours, I'm sure you gave those venture cap guys more than their share of fits."

"Those guys are morons, if you really want to know," I answer. "PlayLouder was never made to be under the microscope for quarterly profits like that. They look at accounting reports, but they don't understand the *soul* that makes it all tick. It's just a matter of time. They can only but fuck up a project like that."

"I can tell just by the way you're talking right now – you don't understand the game. You're not a true businessman at heart."

"What, you have to be an excel sheet myopic office rat to qualify as a businessman nowadays? These guys have never seen the color of a real business from the inside. I'm much more of a real entrepreneur than they will *ever* be."

"Yeah but ... how can I say this nicely," he hesitates. "You're *middle-class* entrepreneur. You still need this irrational connection to what you do. These guys are playing in another league. They look for the big upside. People like you ... you're just the low hanging fruit to them, the guys that keep the wheels spinning."

"Right. I guess that's what you guys pass as capitalism. People with guaranteed salaries who produce nothing and prey on the risk-taking innovators. Revenge of the cowards."

"Charles, it's not about what's right and wrong. What I'm telling you – just ignore it and find a way to bounce back! With your knowledge and contacts, you could become the Ari Gold of the music business! You've got so many friends in the business, you'd probably make more than you ever did at PlayLouder!"

"Yeah, I don't know." I say. "After what I saw last night, I don't think *friends* is the right word to describe the people I know in the industry."

"Whatever, I meant potential business contacts. And look on the bright side, you also have this, like, awesomely hot girlfriend who's totally blowing up as an artist, and...."

"Ex-girlfriend, by the way."

"What? Since when?"

"Three days ago. Anyway, Hal," I get up. "Thanks for everything. I can tell you want to help. I think I just need to be alone for a while."

"No, Charles, I'm staying. We can figure this thing out together! I'll make a call with our wealth management arm, I'm sure they can start by helping you manage what you have now, and ...."

"I appreciate it," I start walking him to the door with insistence. "I'll be in touch, Hal."

"Hey, Charles," he says, halfway out of the door, with a great big insider-type smile. "Good times!" He extends his hand, I shake it and close the door behind him.

I throw myself onto the bed, stretch out. The goddamn press is now in on the madness. But maybe Hal has a point about Prague having fucked me up, though I'd always taken it to be the place where I'd found my life's passion. Maybe that Delta ticket agent had handed me my fate. I need to reconnect to that part of my past that actually meant something to me. Colin, Hal, Ken – even Mandy in her own fucked up way. They may all be speaking to me. And I'd be a fool not to listen.

Chapter 8

"So here, maybe Golem?" the vendor says after failing to catch my interest in a battery of street paintings of the Charles bridge. "Great Jewish statue – just five Euro, just for you!"

"No thanks." I say, and continue speed-walking, in a permanent cringe at the now trendy restaurants and spotless storefronts that make up the heart of Old Town Square. It's not that they're completely new to Prague. But they were once confined to one small city square, a pit-stop of over-priced mousetraps, briefly shielding the vacationers from the surrounding madness. The safe winds of commerce now extend in all directions, purging even the once darkest corners of the city center known as Praha-1. No more decrepit buildings or rusty metal sheets with mysterious post-Soviet poems etched on them. Only the most generic of the English expat graffiti seems to have survived. I feel a bizarre nostalgia for the mayhem, the shadowy winding streets straight out of disturbing fairy tales that kept children up at night, for the cavernous bars in old communist bunkers, for the enlightened wizards disguised as street vendors, telling stories no one wanted to believe but that everyone knew concealed dark, hidden truths. People now seem engaged in all colors of rational, legitimate commerce. They must have locked up the wizards somewhere.

My pre-millennial memories of this place still beat like drums of hope in my chest. The city was at the doorstep of freedom, and the air was electric. The repressed hopes of an unshackled nation mingled promiscuously with democracy's opiate promises. The Soviet bear had finally been slain, and the place was refreshingly lacking in anti-Americanism, that mediocre intellectual crutch that was infecting much of Western Europe at the time. Underground jazz bars were grooving madly to jam sessions and performance poetry, neo-beatniks joined by classically trained locals and seekers from all corners of the old continent. The tectonic plates of history trembled to the beat of hard, industrial techno, below the tired feet of young backpackers, the pimps and petty drug peddlers, and a diverse fauna of wild, fledgling entrepreneurs, all waiting in earnest for an ideal society to emerge from the ashes.

I walk into a convenience store and find some much needed relief in the form of a pink can of Budwar. The best fifty cents on Earth, and enough evidence, for now, to convince me that the advent of what we now blindly pass as freedom hasn't screwed *everything* up.

Next stop Café Slavia, where one can live the culmination of Vaclav Havel's years of dangerous dissident activities and anti-establishment literary efforts: western Europeans hobos carrying shopping bags and overfed babies, yapping busily on their Orange cell phones, flashing earrings that formerly would have been ripped right out of their ears. I close the newspaper I'd opened three minutes ago and quickly gulp a short, burnt and bitter espresso from a shiny Illy cup. The worse five Euros I've ever spent, and my cue to head back to my apartment.

PlayLouder's latest string of e-mails has seen "kind" reminders turn "urgent," "cheers" become "govern yourself accordingly" and "Charles" morph into an ever more formal version of "Mr. Barca." My draft responses have gone from self-redeeming ("*you will fail without me you spineless bastards*") to menacing ("*see you assholes in Court/Hell/record launches*") to cheeky ("*my dog ate my buy-out package*") – but I never bring myself to actually pressing send.

Instead, I spend an inordinate amount of time dwelling on an unexpected e-mail from MIDEM's lead conference organizer:

Hello Mr. Barca:

We hope you are well. We have heard about your recent demission from PlayLouder. But we have always appreciated your contributions in the past, and would like to maintain our relationship with you. I am writing to offer you one of our keynote spots at this year's conference. You could talk about the industry generally, or choose your own topic, which we would have to approve beforehand. Also, we have heard about a new project you may be working on – so for example, we would be thrilled if you wanted to talk about that.

Please e-mail me directly if you have any questions.

Regards,

Anne Leblanc
Conference Organizer, MIDEM

Finally, I reply:

Hello Anne. Thanks for the invite. A "new project" exists about as much as I do right now. Best of luck to you.

"Take me to a place with a lot of people and live music, you know?" I tell the cabdriver as I jump in, a few short minutes after waking up from a heavy, disorienting nap.

"Ah, you want ladies?" he says, two missing teeth punctuating a wicked grin as he cocks his cell phone. "Czech ladies, I find for you, yes? Blonde? Teenage? Yes?"

"No, no teenage, please. Just, you know, a place with good music," I mumble against my best attempt at clarity. "You know, like cave bar with live music and many, many people."

"Yes! I bring you," He smiles broadly and puts up the volume to what sounds like a Czech version of eighties jock rock. He starts driving and rattles off a few text messages. "Lot of ladies for American in Praha!"

I give up my right to reply beyond a sheepish, "haha," figuring the worst that can happen is a welcome stumble away from the beaten path that has apparently swallowed the whole city. We joke around aimlessly for a few minutes, in that foreign traveller patois where neither person understands the other, but both laugh in brotherly approval anyway. Finally, he stops at a busy street corner, framed by luxurious apartments with a battery of Cushman and Wakefield posters hung on their balconies, and a twisting line of tall, looping streetlamps.

He hands me a business card with a construction truck logo on it.

"You nice man," he says. "You call me if need things in Praha. Girls, drink, fixing, okay?"

Fixing?

"Yes, okay," I answer. "I call you for fixing. Thank you."

I get out, turn back and find him staring at me.

"Where?" I ask. He points to a dim street corner with a small green light emanating from the ground. I turn back to him, and he nods furiously.

I walk down the twisting flight of half a dozen stairs and find a small, half-empty bar with three musicians are setting up on a makeshift stage. Not what I was thinking, but I decide to go with it for a bit. I take a seat, order a drink, then another. Between sips, still waiting for the band to start, and while browsing miscellaneous news on my iPhone, I sense a waitress approaching me.

"I'm okay, thanks," I say, waving her off.

"Haha, funny, no," she says, this time placing a firm hand on my shoulder. I look up. She's an attractive dirty blonde, early forties, ruby-red lipstick, long nails, and a black dress slit all the way to the thigh. A creeping feeling hints me that she may not be the waitress.

"Are you here with girlfriend, sitting?" she asks.

"Nope," I say. "No girlfriend for me."

"So I sit?" she says, big grin.

"What?"

"I sit here?" She points to the chair beside me.

"Wha, umm, yeah, okay," I say, realizing there's no real reason for me to refuse. "I mean, sure. Why the heck not."

"So," she says, with an exaggerated, and rather terrible version of a British accent, "what's you name?"

"Charles. You?"

"Dorota. What do you do for live, Charles?"

"What?" I say, wondering whether this is all occurring in my imagination.

"For money. For work, you do for what?"

"Oh, right, money, yes. Well, back home, I'm a famous painter. Like Michelangelo. You know, the Sistine Chapel?"

She lowers her eyes and smiles, or grimaces; I can't really tell.

"What are you drinking?" I ask, choosing to engage the weirdness head-on.

"Oh! Yes! I drink martini. You gentleman!" I surprise myself enjoying her act, her fake, high-minded mannerisms and overdone formality.

"So, this is what Czech women do nowadays? They walk up to strangers in bars hoping to get free drinks?"

"What?"

Forget it.

"So what do *you* do for money, here in Prague?" I ask her.

"I'm writer. Like Rilke. You know, the blind woman?" She looks me straight in the eyes with a smile that betrays an educated irony. Then, she quickly squeezes in closer. "I also know how ... to have good time," she whispers, "with good look man like you."

Her large, cold hands grip mine strongly and her eyes lock in a stare that is both flirtatious and intimidating.

No, I haven't the slightest clue who Rilke's blind woman is. But I'm sure even she can see where this is going.

Dorota's already gone when I wake up, but I'm surprised to see that the small wad of Euros I left for her on my bedside table isn't. I reach for my watch next, in vain. Unfortunately for me, Prague tramps seem to know their luxury accessories from their exchange rates.

I catch a glimpse of my PlayLouder severance package sticking out of my knapsack and notice it now sports a large coffee stain. I feel less intimidated by it now, like I've started to tame it somehow. I get up, take out the sightseeing map and decide that, today, substance abuse will give way to mental substance.

In the great lens of history, racial persecution and good business are apparently not mutually exclusive propositions. Access to the synagogues of the Jewish quarter – a series of glorified gift shops at this point – is now subject to an entry fee of twenty Euros per. I narrowly escape the trap and opt to check out the newly minted Kafka museum instead. Even before I even get there, though, I realize that today's Prague would make old Franz roll over in his sinuous, cockroach-infested grave. T-shirts, coffee mugs, posters, key chains and everything in-between, he's become the city's merchandising equivalent of Mickey fucking Mouse. The museum itself is little more than amateurish recreations of Kafkaesque clichés – tunnels, mazes, winding staircases – and, of course, a bustling souvenir shop as its crown jewel. In three busy generations since his death, Kafka has gone from being banned by Nazis (for being Jewish) to being outlawed by communists (for being a free thinker) to finally being re-appropriated and branded as a local literary cash cow, a kind of Eastern European Che Guevara figure. A true post-modern icon: one that means everything to everyone and, therefore, nothing at all.

In the city's cultural marketplace, Kafka's only rival is the Golem, that mythical clay monster, rumoured – in cryptic tales of lore – to have protected the Jewish community from its Christian persecutors. Key chains, action figurines, teddy bears and statuettes. The Golem sees Kafka's Mickey and raises him an Optimus Prime. A distant residue of national pride briefly squawks for attention in me, as I consider that the ousted Jewish community's symbols are today being pillaged by the descendants of its very tormenters. Instead, walking laconically through the cobbled streets of this now sanitized museum-city, I fail to elaborate a coherent protest to it all. I suppose I expected to find a modicum of transcendence here, something beyond the wheels of business as usual, a sign of things from beyond, a trace of the bohemian soul I'd fallen in love with. Instead, today's Prague strikes me as a disgraced former lady whose husband was killed in the Cold War, deciding to become a high-class whore in order to make ends meet. And yet, she seems in better shape, lighter-footed, better made up, *freer* than she's ever been. In short, a capitalist success story.

Sometimes, the world does unfold logically.

Yahoo! Entertainment's feature of the day: *Feed Me Major - PlayLouder Closes Major Content Deal with Universal.*

Also, Anne Leblanc has answered me:

Mr. Barca:

Thank you for your reply. We fully understand how delicate your current situation must be. We did not mean to be indiscrete! The new project was just an idea ... you could choose any topic you want. The selection committee will naturally defray all costs and you'd obtain the usual VIP access. We hope you will reconsider!

Mandy's daily status update: *Who knew kite-surfing with Peruvian yoga instructors could be so much fun? Namaste ;p.*

Her profile pic showcases her in a white bikini, sporting large Prada sunglasses and holding a fruit drink, small puddles of shiny Hawaiian Tropic suntan oil cradling every heavenly crevice.

I sigh deeply and click on another of Colin's e-mails:

Mr. Barca:

Please be informed that we have just gotten wind of an alleged "new project" of yours. You obviously must know that this violates our existing agreements, which makes us conclude that you must be actively seeking to injure us. Our window to resolve this amicably is getting smaller by the day. I am on vacation until Monday but we are making ourselves free every day next week for you if you wish to take up our offer.

Finally, a missive from Clarice somewhat soothes me:

Charles. I thought you'd have answered by now. I know your head must not be into this. But I have some inside info that could be interesting to you. I write because I truly care. Again, remember please answer on my gmail directly.

Without thinking, I answer Colin:

I'll be there on Tuesday, 1 p.m. Make sure it's an in and out affair

I call the cab driver with the construction logo and leave the money for the rest of the week's rental on the kitchen table. Three days in Prague and I feel dispossessed: of my money, my watch, my time, my heritage, my hope. But most of all, of my favorite dream. Prague. That thieving whore.

Chapter 9

My mother's voice rings more hollow the more the volume of her voice raises.

"I wish you'd never made all that money!" she says on the voicemail. "You ignore me, and why? Just because of that company! You think I care about them? You're in the news and you're NOT answering my messages! Call me!"

I hang up, roll up and light another one. Curtains drawn all the way down, my loft has morphed into a kind of modern Plato's cave: all shadows, reality beaming in from some disfigured imaginary world. Two weeks since Prague have felt rather like months; months of a dead, internal winter, mirroring the view of Montreal I'm getting from the inside.

From time to time, I snap myself into the moment to assess my surroundings, only to find the same languishing mess every time. I reach for memories of my student days for comparison. At least back then, though, I could pretend that my chaotic dwellings were just a pit stop along the way, that the perpetual physical storm that surrounded me was a kind of purgatory, prefiguring a better, more sane, more organized life. But *this* is supposed to be *it*. Bad incense barely concealing the stench of wet hash, Mandy's clothes having been conspicuously moved out while I was away, my green bathroom light turned on for days and nights on end. It all leaves me with no great visions of destiny to latch onto. But maybe I'm missing the point. Maybe this truly *is* it. The logical conclusion of a six-year cycle. A present that no imaginary future can redeem. Reality, uninfected by hope.

I've spent the last few hours wondering who's hiding behind the unusual number of hang-ups on my voicemail. Acquaintances with hidden agendas; desperate artists on the cusp of giving up; PlayLouder cronies seeking to confirm my address; a suicidal friend on his last leg. They all meld together, a multi-faced beast, an infinite library, an undecipherable prism, a world of endless potential knives, twisting deeper and deeper into my rotting mind.

My mother's is the lone voice that pierces through. The person who did so much to shelter me early in life, now the one who needs reality hidden from her. Life just one long cycle of loved ones seeking to protect one another in vain, the strong projecting for the weak the illusion of control over a world in terrifying disorder. That's the end game, it seems. What we strive so hard to become. The meaning of success. To be strong. To be admired. To be eternal. Idols. A bunch of idols, on death row.

I stare at the stack of mail that's been accumulating across the living room – paper, always more and more paper, fertilized by my indifference, growing madly in all directions. On top of one of the stacks, over a dozen unheard demos from artists I'd promised to listen to during my last few hectic months at PlayLouder. I feel for them, laying their souls bare for me to supposedly rescue them, wishing upon stars, crossing fingers earnestly while the big-shot CEO slowly decays in a vortex of meaninglessness.

My buzzer goes off.

"Yes?" I cackle over speaker.

"Charles! My God, I'm so glad you're in!"

"Who's this?"

"Clarice!"

"God ... uhh ... why?"

"Charles, can you please buzz me in?"

Clarice was always the perfect assistant: completely unable to distinguish the importance of the tasks thrown her way. A dry-cleaning mission was executed with the same zeal as setting up a million-dollar closing. She had allowed me to keep my eyes on the big picture, unobstructed by the soul-sucking necessities of daily life. No wonder I'd grown so fond of her.

The light from outside burns through my retina as I open the door. I cover up and slam it shut behind her.

"It's *way* too dark in here," she switches the light on, and gradually comes into focus. She picks some take-out boxes up from the coffee table and puts them into a neat pile on the floor. My living room looks better already.

"Nice to see you," I say, wishing I could manage to sound more sincere.

"So?" she asks, punching my shoulder with a mock smile. "What's up?"

I dim the light and make for the bar. "Drinking anything?"

"It's not even one o'clock," she says, missing the point. She takes a few careful steps in and sits on the edge of my sofa.

"Charles," she says, in a slow, creepy tone, "how can I put this nicely. You don't really have a lot of friends right now."

"Wow!" I say. "Any more earth-shattering news?"

"I'm serious," she continues. "Colin and the new board are telling everyone you're on some kind of kamikaze mission to destroy the company. I mean, you didn't even show up to that closing after you said you would. I keep telling everyone that I know you, that the real Charles wouldn't do anything like that, blah blah blah. But it's not like you're helping me by going AWOL." She frowns when I don't answer her immediately. "I mean, tell me. Am I wrong?"

Feeling reluctant to respond, I pour myself a tall vodka soda and slowly squeeze in half a lime.

"Well?" she asks.

"Well, since we're playing the honesty game, Clarice, I'll let you in on a little secret," I say. "I really don't give much of a damn *what* goes on inside the four walls of that little hellhole. Colin could run for President on a platform of Charles as leader of the axis of evil. Would make no difference in my life. What-so-ever."

"Charles," she flashes an exaggerated look of concern. "I don't think you know what you're getting into." She lowers her voice. "They got a couple of private eyes to confirm you'd been out of the country and talking about a new project. That's what's making them all paranoid about you."

"Private eyes?" I say, pondering that for a few seconds. "Actually Clarice, go back and tell them I was in Prague, chasing the lost spirit of art in the modern world. Instead, I got robbed by a highly-educated prostitute who read me seventeenth century poetry and stole my watch. Go tell them that. I'm sure it'll make them feel just awesome about life in general."

"My God, Charles!" She puts a hand on my forearm. "Are you okay?"

I gently remove her hand. "Look, as far as crimes go, it was of the enjoyable variety, I guess. Anyway, the plan is maybe to swing down to Hawaii next. Or Berlin. Or maybe Thailand. Check out some Thai boxing. Or some cooking classes. Maybe do some of that hang-gliding off a cliff, or go to an all-night rave in the middle of a desert. Something that looks good on a screensaver. Wanna join?"

"Okay, stop it." she says. "I'm serious. The atmosphere's toxic in there. They're firing people left and right. The Mind Ventures people and their lawyers are practically taking over the office."

"Well, that's because the company's busy making all the deals I positioned it for. Read the industry news. You'll see what I'm talking about."

She gives me an exasperated stare. "Okay, I don't know about any of that stuff, Charles. And I don't really care. I just want to know ..." she starts whispering now, "what have you *really* been up to?"

I pause. "Not sure I'm following."

"Since you left ..." her voice gets even lower and more suspicious-sounding, "a lot of us have been talking about joining you and your new project, when it does take off."

I stare back at her blankly for a few seconds, then finally let out a chuckle.

"I see," she says. "There *is* no new project." She shakes her head and looks out of the window. "And they're all in panic mode, thinking you're going to sink them. Fucking Charles."

"See this?" I say, pointing to the swirling sea of chaos in the room. "*This* is the big project I've been working on. Trying to put a foot in front of the next without tripping over a Styrofoam box. And failing, for the most part."

She listens and stays quiet now. In our years together, I can't recall having shared more than the most insignificant personal detail about my life with her. And yet, I'm struck by how those limited interactions have, through accumulation, actually made us understand each other at a deeper level, almost as if by osmosis. I force myself to give her more.

"I don't know what I even *want* out of life anymore," I say. "This whole helping artists thing – what I thought I was living my life for – it was really all just a big hoax, to be honest. Now, everyone's moved on, and I need to do the same. None of it matters, Clarice, right? To each his own, and none of it changes a thing."

"But you've always been so successful," she says, trying to contain her frustration. "I mean, to me, your life was always so glamorous. Even now, you can just do anything you want...."

"Look, everything you know about me is just this super thin veneer of order hiding a world of chaos. Everyone and everything around me, nothing's genuine. It's all just self-serving bullshit. Everyone's just along for the ride. You know what I mean?"

Her expression confirms what I expected. I've lost her.

"So what are you saying?" she asks. "What are you going to do now?"

"No idea, Clarice." I say, pondering this for an instant. "I frankly have no clue."

I wake up to three booming knocks on my door. I rush to open it, and find a three hundred pound mammoth of a man covered in tattoos, with a greying goatee and a tight black T-shirt that covers a rock-hard pot belly, the kind whose abdominal muscles seem to actually lie on top of the fat.

"C'est vous, Charles Barca?" he belts out.

"Oui?" I say, inching backward, bracing myself, trying to regain focus.

"Pour vous." He throws a folded pack of documents at my feet and rushes off.

I turn on a lamp and scour through the documents. A new buyout offer from PlayLouder, with a five-day deadline. I walk to the window and see the beast getting into its small Honda Civic hatchback and racing off.

In the darkness, I slowly regain my senses.

What the hell happened to my fighting spirit? I used to throw looping rights at the status quo, roll with the counter-punches, then go back and swing for more glory. I catch a reflection of myself in the bathroom mirror, growing hairier and fatter and nastier by the minute. These guys took my job, but when the hell did they give me a DNA transplant?

I pick up my phone and SMS Andy, formerly my personal lawyer.

"Well, well, Charlie," Andy says in a slow drawl, suckling a lychee between martini sips and smiling broadly. "You got us in a nice little dill pickle there, haven't you?"

I look around for familiar faces at Garde Manger, an old Montreal hotspot that has become a favourite dwelling place for the city's few business jet-setters, and feel relieved when I don't notice any.

"Glad to see I still amuse you," I say.

He winks. "Always!"

"Here you go guys," the waitress says, as she brings our appetizers.

Andy starts working on his oysters with a passion that can only be attributed to some kind of underlying desperation.

"The spicy tomato sauce here is unreal," he says, consciousness firmly on his fingertips. "I think they've infused it with clam juice or something." His plump cheeks and active hands visually corroborate the stories I've heard of him hitting it big with some of the French indie labels.

"So, what do you think?" I ask.

"About?"

"The friggin' buyout package!"

"Oh, that! Right, yes." He wipes some sauce from his face. "Well, it's pretty standard stuff, except for a couple of things. First, they've actually *increased* the buyout sum from their first offer. Can't figure out why. I mean, they do have you by the proverbial *cojones* with that buy-out clause, which you did sign without my blessing, I might add." He pauses for self-satisfaction. "I mean, I would have never let you...."

"Just continue!"

"Okay. On the other hand, they really want you out of anything even remotely related to music for longer than ever. I mean, after signing this, you won't even be allowed to busk with your guitar in a South African metro station!" He bursts into a hearty laughter, then stops when he notices that I'm not following. "Anyway, the rest is just scary legalese that doesn't mean much. Personally, I'd take the money and run."

"No shit."

"What's that supposed to mean?"

What do you think?

"Andy, I need to know, what's the end game here," I say. "I mean, how do you see this thing playing out?"

"Well, in your shoes, I'd be most worried about that new baby of yours. Maybe that's why they're going nuts on the non-competes and increasing the price. Maybe they want to force your hand and get you wondering what this new project of yours is really worth."

"How many times do I have to tell you ..."

"Yeah, yeah, right, *there is no new project*. Look, there are no buyers for the fact that THE Charles Barca is sitting on his ass counting his unlucky stars. And even if that were God's honest truth, no one would *want* to believe it. I know I don't. The truth is a pathetic shit next to a convincing story. You know that as well as anyone."

"Andy," I sigh in frustration, "my reality may not be all that sexy. But I still need you to be able to deal with it if you want to help."

He collects himself for a few seconds, then starts. "The way I see it, you have two options, broadly speaking. One, you grab the cash and bolt the industry for good. Two, we drag this out and go fishing for something more. But if we do go there, what would we be doing it for, exactly?"

He forces me to think. "To be honest, if you put it that way, I'm not convinced I'm comfortable leaving the industry completely. I mean, I've put everything into this, you know?"

"Interesting." He nods and starts scribbling some notes on the back of the documents. "So the buyout has to reflect not only your leaving the company, but the industry as a whole."

"But it's really not about the money, Andy. I want to find the hunger I once had for this stuff. What I want more than anything is freedom ... just to do what I really want. Whatever it is that happens to be."

"Okay, sure, I get it," he says abruptly. "So, are you putting me on file?"

"Yeah, sure, Andy," I say, down-spirited at his lack of interest, and start clicking on my iPhone. "Threaten, sue, yell. Send them cute letters with scented stamps. Do whatever voodoo it is that you guys do. My head's in the mud right now. I just need time to figure out some things, I guess."

"Loud and clear," he says, and leans back in his chair.

"You know," I say, eyes still down, "they've invited me to speak at Cannes this year."

"What, MIDEM?" he frowns. "Please tell me you're not planning to talk about any of this."

"Don't worry. I've already said no."

As I say this, I look away and notice a group of two model-type girls and a lanky, mulatto guy with blond dreadlocks and an Adidas jacket at a table nearby. I squint, look closer.

"I'll be right back," I tell Andy.

I make toward the bar to get a better look. No question now. It's Mandy. She spots me before I can formulate an adequate game plan, keeps eye contact with me, and gets up from her table. Recovering from a full-body laugh, she walks up to me, offers a toothy smile and beaming eyes. Somehow, we're suddenly body to body in the middle of the packed restaurant.

"Charles! God, how are you babe!" Her attitude clocks in somewhere between condescension and fake concern.

"Good, great, I mean. How are *you* doing?" Fuck.

"My God! This is sooo awkward!" she says, basking in a slow, sexy elegance that's anything but awkward. She glances back toward her table, as if to check that everything is okay with the other two, and turns back at me with an insistent, pitying stare.

"Look, babe," she says, holding both of my hands in a seductive supplication, "I *soooo* have no hard feelings about everything! I mean, life is just too short for grudges, you know?"

"Of course," I say. My mind cuts to my meeting with Colin, then to the moment I learned about our breakup on the world wide web. I now realize I have no fucking clue as to what she means.

"Yeah," I say. "Negative feelings are for losers. Completely."

"I know! People waste so much energy for nothing. Anyway, to be honest, I don't even know *why*, but I did feel bad sometimes." She glances toward her table again. "Like, maybe I should have called, at least one last time? But there was nothing to really say by that point, you know?"

Yup, I nod.

"I like the look with the beard, Charles! Very Guevara!" She looks back again, then caresses the side of my head when she notices the other two aren't watching. "*Awesome*!"

"You don't have to hide you're with that guy," I say. "I get it, and it's fine by me, Mandy."

"Charles, I..." she starts.

Her hesitation imputes me a level of agony I don't actually feel.

"Look, I don't know what to say!" she says. "Just like me and you fell *out* of love, me and him just kinda fell into it I guess. It was just ... natural, I guess."

"Yeah, I know, Mandy," I say. "You're the *it just happens* girl. Always on, always spontaneously connected."

"Hey, don't be a jerk!" She says in that headstrong, haughty voice that instantly reminds me of countless fights. "I mean, we're not even...." She starts whispering in my ear. "If you *really* want to know, me and him, we're not even having sex yet. It's just more ... spiritual with him, I guess."

"Well, to be frank, no I don't really care to know about your sex life, or lack thereof for that matter. And he looks more like Adbuster's idea of a neutered Rasta than a spiritual...."

She stops me. "Charles! My God, you really haven't changed, have you?"

"From what I remember, you're probably the one who needs changing, Mandy." I say, and feel a pang surging up my sinus. "Although I'm sure that a taste of success and two-cent mental makeover later, you probably *feel* very different, but let me tell you, what you did—"

"Charles?" she interrupts.

"Yes?"

"Take my advice. You need to practice detachment," she says and makes some kind of hand gesture in front of my face; a Dr. Spock-like Vulcan salute but with fingers all stuck together.

"What the hell...." I say, pointing to her hand, "what is that thing?"

"I'm at peace with you, okay?"

And, before I can answer, she turns around and makes back to her table. I walk back toward Andy, still confused.

"Hey, Chucky," Andy says in earnest as I take back my seat, "you gonna share the wealth or what?"

"What?" I say.

"Who's the hottie?"

"Just a groupie."

"I want your life."

"Sure you do. Anyway, so where were we?"

"About?"

I pause and look him in the eye, trying to determine whether he really is as unaware as he seems to be about my concerns. Most definitely, yes.

"The oysters, Andy," I stare back toward Mandy's table, where the three of them are laughing splendidly. "Let's get you some more o' them oysters."

I wake up and feel a surge of energy for the first time in weeks. Contract or not, why wouldn't I at least enjoy maybe the last perk the industry wanted to throw at me? Before I get hit by the inevitable drop back down, I fetch my laptop and quickly blurt out an e-mail to Anne Leblanc.

I may be interested in speaking after all. Can't promise you I'll have anything nice to say though ... Let me know

She answers within minutes.

Great news! We'll be sending your speaker's package very soon. Very much looking forward!

Chapter 10

The cool, salty air and bright sunrays wrap around me as I step outside of Nice International Airport. I feel like I've taken a small but discernible step, though I'm still unclear in what direction.

I look around the baggage claim area and my eyes settle on the first unmistakeable sign of MIDEM: a young, energetic man in business-casual attire accompanied by a punkish-looking blonde. Typical music industry couple, I'm thinking – busy-bee manager, appended by the disillusioned artist he's pimping at the moment. He looks sharp in a neatly pressed suit, sporting that networking conference, *business-away-from-business* look: top two shirt buttons undone, trendy sunglasses hanging, pockets presumably bursting with the freshly minted business cards.

The girl, on the other hand, grows unexpectedly more attractive the more I look at her. So much so that, after a couple of minutes, I'm almost over the fact that she's dressed like a two-minute robbery in a thrift store. She's a kind of sexy ballerina caught up in a web of dark, urban-Goth garbs; her strong, flawless Nordic features and deliberate walk giving her an emerging elegance. Her true nature seems to walk half a step behind her consciously designed look – it's almost as though she wishes she weren't as attractive as she naturally is. In a world where most chase images of conventional beauty like fanatics, she seems like one of the few seeking to escape from the real thing.

The suit spots me and winks while jawing on his Blackberry. His body language implies that we know each other – I'm pretty sure we don't. Having packed to the tune of a medium-sized knapsack, I manage to move swiftly past the baggage claim area and toward the exit as I ignore him and peek through window to watch the two interact in an amusing dance of mutual annoyance. He touches her waist slightly; she acquiesces, but reciprocates no affection. He tries for eye contact with me again, and, this time, I have to break it off awkwardly. Watching them, it occurs to me that I'm in Cannes for the first time with no professional purpose in mind. I feel liberated from the shackles of business, and a clean breath of air infuses through me as I walk toward the bus stand.

On the 5:30 bus to Cannes, I take my *Lolita* book, bag, iPad and newspaper and sprawl them evenly on the seat to my left, making my antisocial intentions known to all oncomers. The bus is half empty when the two walk in, but he brushes past her and takes the seat directly in front of mine. I plug in my earpiece, turn to the window, and open my book to push his attention away. Just as I slip into a deliciously disturbing passage about nymphets in schoolyards, he turns and taps my arm.

"Hello, sir! I'm Lothar Tykwer! And this," he points to the girl, "this is my very good friend and client DJ Minima!" His speech, with its heavy German inflexions, is energetic and methodical, almost convincing enough to sound un-rehearsed.

"I'm her European tour manager," he continues. "So, I guess you are here for the MIDEM?"

His eyes glow expectantly, angling for the kind of respect that would come from me knowing who they are, which I don't.

"No, actually not," I answer, barely squeezing out my voice. "Just here ... on vacation."

"Oh," he says, looking puzzled. "You are not Mister Barca?"

"No!" I say, attempting not to erupt into a full-face flush. I look away, but he stays put.

"Oh, okay, sir, I am sorry. Because we were thinking, you look like someone we know in our industry. Right, Mini?"

The girl ekes out an ironic half-smile, barely concealing her boredom. Her rebellious introversion is typical of a certain sub-category of successful underground artists whose even more successful managers don't listen to a word they say.

Meanwhile, he stays intensely fixated on me. I'm almost certain he's onto my mediocre little act by now. This can't be happening, I'm thinking. Not yet, not with a guy like this. There's no upside to *this* kind of fame.

"Don't worry about it," I finally say, trying to casually break an awkward pause. "I'm always mistaken for being someone I'm not." I quickly angle back to my book, hoping not to give him any more clean looks.

"Well, sorry again, sir," he says, suspiciously. "So, you don't work in music at all?"

"No. Finance, actually," I offer, in as clear a fuck-off move as I can muster. "I deal in commodities. Like precious metals, crude, cereal. Speculate on the fluctuations. Term contract trading. You know, stuff like that."

"Cereal?" he answers.

"Yup. Cereal. Like … wheat," I say, eyes dropping down toward my book but not reading. "It's pretty big."

I can see his head still hanging on top of his seat from the corner of my eyes. "So anyway," I continue, "investors – and I mean, the big guys – yeah, they aren't really touching music anymore, are they? But I'm sure that with a go-getting little whippersnapper like you representing them," I get up a little bit and point my stare toward the girl, "*your* artists really have nothing to worry about!"

She shoots a glance of curious approval toward me, but Lothar's tireless Bavarian babble keeps bobbing on.

"Wow, that is interesting," he says, undeterred, "but we aren't very dependent on the market, are we, Mini? Our label is *Blatnoi* records, yes, and it's fully funded by a Russian jetsetter millionaire. We get full funding for everything! As long as his entourage and models love it, he has fun with it, everyone gets paid, always. He doesn't care if he loses money! So this is not our problems, right, Mini?"

She smiles weakly.

"So, anyway, where are you from?" he asks.

"Canada. Montreal, actually." And the armour is cracked.

"Funny, well, we love Montreal, don't we, Mini? One of our biggest fan-base is there. And even the person we thought you were is from there. Coincidences! Actually, we are playing at a Montreal club called, what again? Berry or something? In February. Here," he says, and hands me a business card with his name under a red logo for ACTIV MANAGEMENT.

"Who knows, maybe we see each other there?" he says.

"Yeah," I reply hesitantly, "maybe we do." He gives me a parting smile and finally lets me off the hook. Mini looks at me for a few couple of extra seconds, with a slightly subdued smile, the kind that makes her appear both shy and supremely confident at the same time. Lothar's paying no attention to her, and is already thumb-typing away to grand feats of business acrobatics, no doubt. Two world wars, I'm thinking, for this. The right of Germans to turn into East Coast style business scum. *This* is the industry I'm struggling to stay a part of.

I try to retain eye contact with her for another moment, in vain.

Then, I turn my attention out toward the flat green panorama all around us, stretching to and from the blue slits of the North Mediterranean. The air seeping into the bus is cool and crisp, sustaining a subtle, satisfying fatigue in me, as I take in the buzzing road to a quiet sense of contentment.

My suite at the Majestic Hotel brings me face to face with the stylish futility of my life's pursuits. Groucho Marx was right: money doesn't make you happy – it just allows you to pick your misery. I open an envelope that's placed on top of my conference package. It's from Ken Brand.

> *Mr. Charles! You can imagine how pleased I was when I heard you would be speaking this year. To get things broken in with style, my people are inviting you to an exclusive party tomorrow night at Chokko. You're on Big Benjamin's list + 1. Looking forward to seeing you there, KB.*

I experience a brief moment of gratitude for all the people who still have delusions as to who I "am." I walk onto the balcony and start jotting down some notes for my keynote.

What can be said when the apocalypse descends on the deserving? When sixteen year olds spun the technology that would sink them, the majors turned to two types of experts. First up were those who got paid to build ever more detailed versions of the "messianic system that would save the industry." From tech gurus to marketing whizzes, Ivy League consultants and wise old industry dogs, they took turns selling the industry the false dream that new gimmicks could somehow re-create the past. On the other end of the spectrum were the realists: the managers, administrators, the systems-tweakers, those focused on the last quarter's results. These more realist types turned to dark diagnostics and short-term remedies. Slashing superfluous staff, finding new targets for lawsuits, focusing on the immediate bread-winners, dumping artist development altogether, finding more efficient ways to manage the back catalogue. The false prophets and the trigger-happy surgeons. The former selling the dying tyrant dreams of future conquests, the latter keeping him on life support for a few more miserable years.

Historically, developments in the music market have seemed to predict larger social trends: the great public concerts of the Renaissance announced the new bourgeoisie's need for entertainment and the free marketplace; the rise of recordings in the nineteenth century foreshadowed the mass marketing of reproducible objects; the improvisational ideal of jazz in the twenties prefigured the youth rebellion of the sixties. If the trend keeps up, the iPod nation predicts an age of autistic individuality, where shared culture is replaced by the self-determined consumption of atomized individuals devoid of any social consciousness. Meanwhile, the death of the major labels may tell us much about how large, post-industrial institutions behave when faced with existential threats: with a schizophrenic dementia equal parts melancholy and blind violence. Maybe what's happening in music is a kind of harbinger for what will happen next in western civilization. What a buzz kill.

My mind starts drifting to the countless advantages of just skipping the whole thing – speech, industry drama, all the illusory mess in between. Just go walk around, enjoy whatever goodie I can fetch, go back home on a whim whenever I feel like it. In the past there was always a greater responsibility, a larger reason justifying every personal compromise. I'd always assumed there was a grand purpose behind everything. Maybe that was the problem. All that misplaced heroism. All those hopeful fabrications. Maybe the key to life lies in losing the ideals that turn us to sacrifice.

Chapter 11

I spot him from afar as soon as I step out of my room and into the Palais des Festivals area. Colin, along with Nick, my marketing director, and two others I don't recognize.

I can't be surprised they're at MIDEM. Not as they've just partnered up with the industry's 2,000-pound gorilla. My fragile sense of cool leaves almost instantly as I rove parallel to them, disappointed that I can't bring myself to feel the indifference they deserve.

Finally, I lunge in front of Colin and extend my hand in earnest.

"Colin!"

He frowns and takes a step back.

"Charles!" Nick says with a warm, spontaneous smile. "Did *not* think I'd see you here!"

He turns to the two unknowns, pointing to me. "Guys, this is the man who started it all. Pretty much invented everything we do every day. Right, Colin?"

Colin stays quiet behind a perplexed expression. "Good to see you, Charles. Nick is right, what *are* you doing here?"

"Keynote," I offer, slowly settling down. "You look different, Colin. There's a color in your face that's ... new."

"Well, becoming CEO can have that effect on someone, no?" Nick says, jokingly, as the unknowns watch on.

"You never showed up to that closing, Charles," Colin continues, abruptly. "We spent significant sums setting that up."

"Yeah, sorry about that," I say. "I think I had volleyball practice that day or something."

Nick lets out a muffled laugh, as Colin icily stares him down.

"Well, why don't we set one up while we're all here?" Colin asks. The two-some whip out their Blackberries, ready to pound another item into their schedules.

"Not doing meetings this year, Colin," I answer. "I'm here on ... well, let's just say other business."

"What business?" he snaps back. I feel a short, mediocre pulse of self-satisfaction. I always had a better poker face than him.

"Not at liberty to talk about it, buddy. Anyway, I'm sure we'll be seeing each other at some of the parties, right guys? You're the stars and we're just the audience!" I shake hands with everyone except Colin, then turn to Nick. "Good luck, man. I mean it."

"Well, then," Colin interjects, "I'm sure you are aware that any *business* of yours would fall under our non-compete. We could stop you by injunction and significantly complicate your life. Your lawyer must have explained that to you."

I pause, unsure what to answer.

"But anyway," he continues, starting to turn away with the others following, "I'm sure we'll be in touch soon through counsel. Enjoy Cannes, Charles."

They take a few steps out, and Nick turns back briefly, flashing an expression of sincere apology. I nod, disgust visible, and twist away toward the well-groomed green pathway in front of me.

Small groups are congregating outside of Chokko, the black light beams and cigarette smoke painting their silhouettes as blue phantoms in an ashy cloud. Walking alone and catching bits of conversations in different languages, watching the people gesticulate expertly to one another, I realize that Europe isn't any less superficial than America is; its charm, rather, lies in making that same superficiality infinitely more seductive. People slowly trickle into the club, and the clear woof of deep house bass lines emanates outward in smooth, concentric waves. I feel liberated, although not sure exactly of what. Maybe of an excessive expectation of fulfillment in this world. Looking around for Ken and his group in vain, I seek out someone to break the ice with, and stop by a group of two young guys in narrow suits and a slim, attractive brunette wearing an open-busted black dress and a red satin scarf wrapped around her shoulders.

"Hey," I interrupt one of the guys mid-sentence, "mind if I bum a smoke?"

"Sure," one of them says, handing me one.

"Where are you from?" the other guy asks. The girl is giving her best impression of bored, gazing impatiently from side to side as I light up.

"Montreal," I say, taking a long drag. "Charles, by the way." I shake their hands, ignoring hers.

"I'm Johan. And this is Henry," the first one says.

"Selena," the girl now says, through a fake polite smile.

"So who's your ticket in here?" Henry says, in a fast, cutting British twang.

"Dependable friends in low places, I guess," I answer. We share a small laugh while Selena smiles, almost completely to herself.

"Likewise here!" Johan says. "So what part of the business are you in?"

"The newly retired one," I say, hoping to steer clear of the drudgery of industry babble. "It's the fastest growing segment, actually. You?"

The guys are unsure how to react, but the girl seems amused. By the time Jonas starts answering, we've already exchanged furtive stares.

"We're all with Warner." He pauses, pausing to give me the opportunity to be amazed. "Myself in Stockholm, Henry in London, Selena in New York. We're all in marketing."

"So, who invites retired geezers to events like these nowadays?" Henry asks, as Johan evasively hands him a couple of capsules.

I can't help but let out a muffled, heartfelt laugh. My last couple of years at PlayLouder had been spent hanging out with an older, more connected crowd. People like these three, whose claims to being more "fun and genuine" were born, I was certain of it, out of failure and impotence, were useless to me, part of an irrelevant underclass I'd left behind in my blazing tracks.

"Grammy-winning hip hop moguls. Who else?" I answer. They giggle at the same time, like a group who gets that feeling of mutual understanding for the first time. "Now there's also something I want to know." They pause attentively. "Were you guys really about to leave Selena and I out of the fun?"

"What are you talking about?" Jonas says, looking at Henry defensively.

"Yeah, Charles, what *are* you talking about?" Selena asks, amused.

"No really, seriously, what are you saying?" Henry says, turning me into the stranger again, punching himself out of the corner like any good Brit would.

"Come on, guys. You may as well wear Energizer Bunny T-shirts and stink of Vicks Vaporub. I have built-in night vision for those things."

They look at me incredulously. Henry immediately smiles like he just got red-handed shoplifting a piece of candy.

"So what are we talking exactly?" I ask.

"Hey, we may be working with a major, but we know our pills from our capsules." Henry says. "The pure thing, of course."

"Nice," I say. "So you *were* locking us out, right?"

"Hey, hey," Henry says. "We just weren't comfortable corrupting senior citizens," he says. "Not to mention innocent young American princesses."

Jonas jumps in. "We do have one left. Here," he hands me a little twist-on capsule.

"Shall we go in?" I say, walking slightly ahead of the group, as they follow me swiftly into the club.

We walk up the narrow staircase leading into the club, a square maze in almost complete darkness, with shades of red and purple lights illuminating its corners. It immediately strikes me as a great place to disappear in, were it not from the industry eyeballs ogling at me tangibly. I head straight to the bar, not turning back to see whether they're following, order a water bottle, discreetly twist in my capsule.

"We're gonna walk around a bit," Johan tells Selena, Henry following him. "Lots of important players around."

She nods and slides her hand down my arm.

"May I?" she whispers into my ear, and grabs the bottle from me. I look at her, surprised. "Right, look," she continues, "I've a rep to keep as the workaholic American princess with these guys."

She takes in a large swig of water and hands it back to me. I'm shocked at her being so up front, especially as she'd dropped almost no hints until then. I gulp down most of the rest, leaving her one last sip.

"Really?" I say.

"Yeah," she smiles and gives me a wet peck on the edge of my mouth. "We're good."

I turn, run my hand down her arm slightly and take the music in, waiting giddily for the buzz to kick in.

"Can I ask you a question?" she asks, holding a flirtatious look.

"Sure, go ahead."

"I've kind of been following the industry news a little. Aren't you that guy from PlayLouder?"

"Ya, yes, but I'm not here..." I stumble, as I get tapped from behind, mercifully bailing me out of having to come up with an intelligible answer.

"Mr. Barca?" A short, balding mid-aged man with a goatee screams in my ear, cutting through the loud music.

"Yes?" I answer.

"Johnny Meyer. Formerly Sony A&R. Hiring?"

"What?" I scream back, barely making out the sounds coming from him.

"HIRING!" he yells. "ARE YOU HIRING?" He pauses slightly as he utters each syllable.

"What? No, no, man, not hiring. I'm on welfare, too! Let's party!" I smile, expecting him to follow. His eyes remain steely and distant, and his hand is now firmly planted on my shoulder as he dips his face deep into my neck.

"Look man, I know you're used to everyone kissing your ass," he huffs out with purpose. "King o' the fuckin' indies. But I," he centers back in front of me, fixing my eyes squarely, "*I*," he repeats, "am your real legacy. Me and all my A and R guys got fired because of PlayLouder. You know, us, the dummies, the guys who actually went to the clubs, met the bands, loved the music. We're all gone now, selling insurance, telemarketing, God knows what the fuck else. That's what you guys really did. Took the only people who cared about the talent out of the picture. Took the music," he pauses, almost for dramatic effect, then crisply snapps the middle finger and thumb of his large, furry hand in front of my nose, "right out of the industry."

I try to turn away, but stay fixated on him instead. His aggression is almost completely gone now, like he'd discharged himself of a great burden. I stay tuned in, unable to snap away from his gaze for a few seconds.

"I'm ... sorry. I.... We were ..."

But nothing coherent makes its way out. The real answer is I couldn't have given a smaller shit about the antiquated Artist and Repertoire model he'd operated under when I was running things. In fact, I had actively sought to destroy it. Why should I have cared about major label employees, locked, for whatever reason, in an inefficient system for locating talent? They had unfairly benefited from their own bubble of unrealistic wealth during the nineties CD boom. But this is the first time my own eyes see that my legacy has been, in large part, been about replacing music-loving humans with executable software. I'd been predatory and proud of it, taught not only to be indifferent to those with competing agendas, but to have a pompous disdain for them.

"You're right, I...." I would have probably stayed there for several more seconds had Selena not taken my hand and tugged me back toward her.

She grabs my face with both hands. "What's going on? You look like you've seen a ghost!"

"I have, I...."

She bursts out laughing.

A soft tingle hits my cheeks, reaching its apex in a wave of warmth that flushes through my crane and chest at the same time.

"Who, that guy?" she asks, looking in his direction. "Hiiii!" She waves a hand toward him.

He raises his beer stoically and holds a firm stare at her.

She dismisses him with nonchalant grace and turns back to me, body to body now. "Come *on*, Charles!" she says, eyes glowing, gently pressing against me. "He's so ... cute!"

"No, he's just Sony and ..." My own slurring distracts me, "I.... well, my former company.... we ..."

She looks at me almost admiringly, though I can't figure out why.

"You look ... happy," I say, finally.

"Can I be honest?" she says.

I nod.

"Come."

She leads me to the dance floor, which is almost completely empty. People are mostly standing around the bar area, looking sharp, staring at us like owls with night vision. None of it matters, though. The influx of positivity is anchored in me hormonally now, serotonin-infused angels flooding my system freely. My eyes only catch fleeting glimpses of her, frame by frame, a succession of angular shadows projected at me by the blue strobe light. For an instant, the future seems open again. Her hair cascades down her shoulders. I get closer; she flashes a kind of weak, ill-fated protest, then closes her eyes and moves toward me again, slower and steadier this time. I take her hand and lead her to a corner of the club, nestled deep behind the DJ booth. She opens her lips slightly. We close our eyes, everything disappears.

My mind wanders to that couple of years in the nineties when I'd progressively decided to dedicate my life to giving the creators of sonic beauty a worldly platform. In the West, walls were crumbling and hope was rising. Strangers fell deeply in love for no reason. For a few short years, everything was possible. A cute idea would quickly butterfly into an eighty million dollar IPO. Ethnic differences fed sexual curiosities rather than military conflicts. DJ's became high priests, spinning wordless beats, awakening the gods of universal humanity, leaving jealous tribal deities impotent in their wake. It would only be a few years, no doubt, before war and greed became obsolete. Digital utopia promised that art would wiggle free from the stranglehold of corporatism and meld into a worldwide revolution of the spirit. Millions of MDMA capsules would drop into the Middle East's rivers and, before long, Israelis and Palestinians would wave olive branches at each other like glow-sticks, deserts turning into playgrounds for week-long raves, peace treaties signed in orgiastic fervour. The most compelling question of the times was: *why not?* I certainly wasn't getting in the way. In fact, I'd start my own revolutionary cell, and make a living doing it.

I press her hard against the wall. Just as my hand snakes down her bare waist, she grabs my wrist and pushes me away.

"Stop! We have to stop," she says, still in an obvious state of pleasure, but wresting herself away from me. "Not like this, Charles ... not now."

"Wha.... Just ... relax ..." I offer weakly.

"I can't. We ... we can't do this. I'm ... not ... like this...." She takes a few flustered steps back.

I remember how quickly those dreams were done away with. Somewhere between the W Bush election and the war on terror, after September 11, but definitely before the war in Iraq, reality made a comeback, and would take no prisoners this time. Bubbles burst, new walls were erected. Church bells rang. New evils were sought, found, fought, invented. Hope became obsolete.

As I watch Selena walking away, the music in my head gradually fades. My eyes follow her at first, then lose her in the thickening crowd. My mouth is dry. I turn once around myself completely. She's gone now. All that remains are the stares of an inexplicably sober crowd, digging in on me ruthlessly from all angles. My buzz turns sour as quickly as it did sweet. A large hand palms my shoulder from behind.

"My man!" Ken says, and hugs me warmly.

I feel an impulse of anger. I take a deep breath in, refocus on him.

"Why did you have to do that, man?" I ask.

He turns to a serious stare.

"What?"

"The rumours, man. Why'd you talk about things so much?"

"What rumours? Your project?" he asks.

"Yes, my supposed project. The one that doesn't exist. Yeah, that one."

"Doesn't exist? So you mean you ... *lied* when you....?"

"I ... " I start, only now realizing he had no reason to know of my idiotic deceptiveness at the time, " ... was wasted and just got canned. Anyway, you know, you put me in a bad spot with a lot of people. Fact is, I'm kinda done with the industry now, and PlayLouder's getting ready to sue me into oblivion, and I have fucking MIDEM people everywhere talking about it. It's a big fucking mess, Ken."

"Hey, come on, Charlie, you know how it gets!" He starts laughing warmly. "You can't control your news in this business! But let me tell you what I *have* been hearin' from *everyone*," he continues, impervious to everything I've just told him. "You're hot stock, Chucky. Maybe the hottest in the whole biz. I'm sure your former employers are feeling the heat right about now. 'Cause word is, you are *the* man all the big boys are angling for in Cannes this year. Trust me."

Chapter 12

I wake up to a pounding head and dry mouth, clothes still on from last night. I gulp a warm glass of water and pull out the stack of business cards from my pants pocket. Eleven of them, not one memory from the people they're from. Selena's isn't one of them.

I open my notepad to try and prepare some notes for my speech tonight. Every word of it weighs on me like death. I click on Facebook instead. Mandy's status: *cradling civilization*, an album of fifty eight pictures of her in South Africa with her new Yogi boyfriend. I send an e-mail to Andy: "*Cannes a bust. Talk soon in Mtl. CB.*"

Call us if we can help you with anything, the personalized letter on top of my conference package reads.

"Hello, Anne?"

"Charles! How are you enjoying yourself?" she asks, curtly, as though in the middle of an intricate juggling act.

"I don't know how to say this, but ... could you guys possibly find a replacement for tonight?"

"Mr. Barca!" she exclaims, switching to formality. "What … why?"

"Look, I feel terrible, but is it possible?"

"Fuck! No, it's not!"

The word "fuck" is so much more intimidating when said out of place, and with a Swiss-German accent.

"Look, I'm already sort of forced to be out of the business as it is. I have more enemies than friends out here. If anything, it'll be an embarrassment for all of us."

"You cannot do this!" she yells, then slows herself down. "I mean, can we do *anything* to make you more comfortable?"

"I don't think so, I just ... don't see the point anymore, to be honest."

"Okay, now, listen," she says, "you cannot do this. Not on the day of the speech. I mean, not for no valid medical reason. You're in one of our prime positions. The buzz from your talk is enormous. People are calling, asking about your topic, but we've given you more flexibility than the others because of your past...."

"I know, I'm sorry Anne. But I don't think you're listening to me. I'm leaving the *whole industry* behind. I'll pay you guys back for everything, of course."

"This is not about money, Mr. Barca!" she interjects. "Okay, I understand you, but it's a keynote. It doesn't have to be a self-promotional thing. If you want to leave the industry, why not just tell everyone why? In a way, you can just be honest and not care what people think."

Her words ring like a deafening bell of truth to my tired ears.

"Anne, I get you too, I just...." I look around at my executive room, full of all the luxuries money can buy, which brings my sense of self-ridicule to fever pitch. "Okay ... we'll see."

"No," she answers, "we need more than we'll see. We are the day of. It may be a swan song for you, but it's our business here."

Swan song?

I sigh. "I can't guarantee anything good."

"We never ask for that. See you at six?"

The amphitheatre is packed, with new bodies still trickling in just a few moments after the break. The first two keynotes, "Monetizing e-music" by a panel of major label executives, and "DJ's vs. Pirates," a question and answer between Chuck Klosterman and Billboard producer of the decade, Pharrell, have generated the usual low-fi banter and conventional questions from the audience. I'm the third, and last, the audience will hear tonight. I see the plan now. I'm supposed to tie it all together before people head back into the bazaar of networking and jostling. Not a bad one. On paper.

"Okay, everyone, we're going to get things re-started here," says Eric McGuinness, the conference moderator, from behind the main podium.

I'm sitting on a chair in the middle of the stage, with a large, empty blue screen behind me, on which I know no snazzy PowerPoint or video will materialize to the rescue. I shuffle my two pages of scribbled notes in search of a starting sentence, but none has come up yet.

"Our last, but definitely not least, speaker tonight is Charles Barca," Eric continues. "Many lay claim to the title, but Charles is truly a pioneer of the *new* music industry. Few have navigated the new technological reality the way he has, even fewer with as much success. He founded PlayLouder in 2005. The rest, as they say, is history. He's since left his brainchild, for greener pastures we must assume!" He pauses slightly and a low, rumbling murmur runs through the crowd.

"His ideas are always at the very cutting edge, and he's proved time and again that when he speaks, the rest of us should grab the notepads and get out of the way. Everyone, please welcome, Charles Barca."

He turns and points for me to join him at the podium. Polite, underwhelming applause starts, then stops suddenly.

I look around and take a deep look at the sea of faces in front of me. Many of them are familiar, some painfully so. "Thanks Eric." My eyes scatter for the couple of lame first lines I had jotted when I seize up, unable to start.

"Oh, and excuse me!" Eric interjects. "Sorry, Charles, I forgot one last thing. You guys can now download the new MIDEM application on your smart phones," he says to the audience. "We'll be making regular feeds on it throughout the rest of the conference. That's the new industry for you, right, Charles? Ha!"

I smile back. The room loosens up, and so do I.

"The floor is yours," he says.

The crowd is now chattering and chuckling, but their eyes are not dead fixed on me anymore.

"You see ..." I say, clearing my throat, taking in a deep breath, "that's probably part of the *problem* right there." I point to Eric. He forces a puzzled smile back at me.

"There's a word I keep hearing when you guys talk about anything *di-gi-tal*." I say, exaggerating each syllable. "And that's the word *new*."

The collective gaze falls intently on me. Time slows down. My trembling hands let loose of my scribbled notes. I stretch out, making myself a bit larger in front of the crowd.

"AOL was founded over twenty five years ago. Zuckerberg hadn't said his first brilliantly manipulative words. Lady Gaga wasn't even born. Let's face it. There's nothing *new* about digital. The dot-com boom and bust? The end of the cold war? The Clinton years? The goddamn *Internet*? That was over two decades ago, guys. Show me someone who can't stop talking about the *new* and I'll show you someone still part of the *old*."

Petty, mocking laughter makes its way throughout the audience. I stop and relax, as my ideas are getting clearer.

"The only really new thing is that people now realize how little value people like us have. Marketing, administration, pushing the paper, making the phone calls. This whole vast, self-appointed bureaucracy of office peddling. We don't even come close to the ninety percent we've hoarded historically. That could only be justified when the large up-front financing was needed and the big sales numbers were still possible. Today, the whole package may be worth as little as ten, maybe fifteen points on the dollar. That means we still have a long way down to go, guys, before our *price* accurately reflects our *value*." I hear a few giggles, see people smirking and whispering to each other, but I find the words coming out effortlessly now.

"In reality, we, the non-musicians, easily forget that music precedes the commercial arrangements used for its distribution. People made music before money even existed, and today people continue to do so even as copyright becomes a joke. The only perishable thing in the long run is the system through which the people who *don't* make the music vampirize those who do. Their stranglehold is, and always has been, a temporary one, tied up to the economic ebbs and flows of the day."

The chatter is getting a bit louder, but subsides as I start again.

"Truth is, the post-war music system is dead, and it's not even that big of a deal. Great empires have crumbled before it, and greater ones will die after it. We worked hard to turn music into this complex technical product to artificially inflate its value, and the consumer bought it for a while. In a way, the whole twentieth century record industry model was just a brief bubble in time we can start calling *music as plastic*. Vinyls, tapes, and discs. That's it, really, when you think about it. A perfect storm for music capitalism. Only free markets don't stop at perfection. The system drives eternally on like a voracious inferno. Music as plastic had *some* value, I guess. But when you think about it, supposedly free music actually means a lot more money for a lot more people. Whether it's on Internet service, computers, iPods, mobile phone bills, or Apps, add it all up, and consumers have never paid more to get access to their distractions. And yet, they're also more *satisfied* because they get the illusion of free content. One of the greatest illusions of all time. That's the real genius here. The techies convinced everyone this was a Robin Hood act by a bunch of adorable geeks when, in truth, it was a Houdini by bona fide whiz kids. Well then, the least you can do is be gracious in defeat instead of continuing to throw these ridiculous celebrations. You guys have become the dancing idiot at his own funeral." Some people are now talking openly, which forces me to pause, before I decide to continue on.

"Well, the revenge of the nerds is now complete. The devaluation of music is a permanent phenomenon. It's a new information Darwinism out there, and it's the day after the end of the world. The leaders among you still speak the language of law and order, as though everything would go back to normal if only everyone respected the *rules*. But a rule is just power gone justified. On the law-making front, the ISP and telecom and computer lobbies just ran you over like the political lightweights you are. What happened to music isn't a result of society's rules being broken. Rather, it's an exact reflection of those very rules. God is dead. The grownups are selfish and corrupt. The law is the strong man's iron fist. And justice is the impotent cry of the dispossessed."

The room is entirely quiet all of a sudden. I've completely let go of my notes, and am simply addressing the crowd directly now.

"The really suspect thing, though, is that I've seen no fear in anyone's eyes here in Cannes. No panic button seems to have been pressed with any of you. No deeper instinct of survival has kicked in. I think what may have happened in music in the last few years is a kind of reverse natural selection. The strong ones, those with the fight in them, tried to confront the looming threats head on. But since they didn't – in fact, *couldn't* – win the war, they ended up losing their credibility, their minds, and, finally, their jobs.

"The ones who've survived the music apocalypse are the passive ones, the silent and weak-minded administrators. Those attached to the system for their own self-preservation only. To keep the seat warm at the office on Monday morning. Those most likely to accept the enemy as their new master. In the music industry, your long term chances of survival seem to be directly proportional to your level of cowardice."

I notice a few more people talking into each other's ears – but their reactions don't matter anymore, and I figure I've still got a few more minutes.

"And so, the majors will continue to merge and centralize until they're all owned by some combination of Google, Apple, maybe some state-sponsored Asian conglomerates. Do you seriously not see this coming? They'll end up focusing on big, bubble pop and catalogue management almost exclusively. Staffers will be mostly slashed, the managerial class down to a few systems operators. In these new, ruthless structures, the creative human being will become a useless redundancy. Those of you who persist to stay in the music business will be forced to become part of smaller companies that won't provide the kind of stable, health benefit and pension-appended jobs that you crave. So you'll naturally let go and take jobs with the same titles, but in other industries. In the long run, what is happening is probably a great flushing system. Those not truly in it for the love of music will slowly weed themselves out."

"As for me," I continue, "I know everyone's been hearing rumours since PlayLouder's been high-jacked by our investors. MIDEM invited me this year to talk about a quote on quote *new project*. Truth is, there is no new project. And there won't be one, either. I'll admit to being slightly nuts, but not nearly enough to throw good money after bad in the present state of the industry. But I'll be a good sport and tell you what I would do if I *were* in your shoes, which, thanks for me, I most definitely am not."

People's faces have now become more serious, heads are supported by hands, facial expressions are sobering.

"When facing a revolution," I continue, "one must act in revolutionary ways. Going with the flow means draining down the sinkhole. So if I did it, I'd strip down everything legit to business-to-business transactions, and take the rest of the show completely underground. Insane times call for creative forms of organized crime, and, if I did it, I'd have been the Joker on a massive crime binge. Robbery, kidnapping, targeted killings, espionage. Whatever works. The future is not in defeating the illegal market, but in becoming the new don of the digital underworld. And if I did it I'd come out Uzis a-blazing, pulling mafia stunts on the street punks who are dictating the rules of the game. I'd have systems spun that would make the Napsters and Limewires look like children fumbling with toys.

"At their root, your failures are not legal or even technological, but simply of imagination and good old guts. The enemy wants to fight dirty? Fine. I'd copy their technology and snatch all the web dollars I could with illegal sites. I'd invest in technology that tracks every whim of the mind, and in branding that attracts the masses like zombies. The techies raped you twice: first by inventing file-sharing, second by charging you billions for technology that, in some make-believe world, was supposed to lock up your digital files. So, if it were up to me I'd take the major tech companies and completely rip their back ends, spray paint my skins in pink and pretend the whole thing was the wet dream of a fourteen-year-old Asian whiz kid who doesn't exist. I'd rip mix and burn my way to hell and back. And if a site didn't stick in ninety days, I'd spin the whole thing back into next month's flavour. And I'd run it all like a black cloud, a bad dream of bandwidth and software that didn't belong to me. I'd pimp whatever generates however much cash for however long as it would. And I'd do it like Maradona's hand of God, scoring by breaking the rules, my excuse being that *I've only stolen from a thief.* At the end of the day, all great human institutions are built on a mountain of small, hidden crimes. The ISP and hardware industries are hoodwinking everyone into not seeing that their skyrocketing valuations are largely based on the content being free. Is it fair? No. But it's still happening. The age-old formula of all great businesses says it does. Comply only when compelled, find loopholes where possible, change the facts on the ground, and negotiate your way out of any real trouble using the spoils of war. But, if I did it, there's one thing I would know for fact. If the cyberspace is really going to be a lawless frontier, if the *world-wide-web* actually stands for *wild-wild-west*, then I'm either a law-obedient victim or the baddest outlaw in town. Sabotage? Hidden identities? Offshore servers in war-torn African countries? I don't even know what I'd do, but I know I'd have no limits. And I wouldn't hire low testosterone academics or smug economists as my consultants. I'd go for retired CIA agents and arms manufacturers and al-Qaeda operatives.

"But most of you probably don't even care what happens to the industry. That's because you're just a collection of disconnected managers and employees, in the game for salaries and personal perks, sucking the dying animal's blood as much as anyone else. And maybe that's a decent personal strategy for you, after all. I just pity the state of this industry, as it seems to be standing on the shoulders of midgets. But I certainly don't care. Because I'm not in your position. And I never will be."

I stop, take a breath. My face is red, I calm down for an instant, look around. People are turning to each other, whispering, sneering.

"Because, as I've said," I say, "I'm *not* doing it. Not now, not ever. I could have fought to keep my position. But the war is over when there's nothing left to fight for. I built a small fortune being one little step ahead of you guys, which, by the way, wasn't too fucking hard."

I step away from the podium, toward the staircase leading from the podium to the floor, and yell, "I'm out. Don't believe any of it. Good luck and goodbye."

Eyes stare at me wide open as I focus on the exit. The whole thing doubtlessly would have been more satisfying had I not slightly tripped on the microphone stand, causing a dull thud to resonate throughout the room. A few scattered applauses are drowned by a low chatter, swelling up like an animated midnight sea.

"Wow, thank you. Thanks for this, Charles. I'm sure there are lots of questions," Eric says into the microphone, just as I approach the exit door.

I stop, raise my hand to say, "No," and walk out the door, all eyes on me.

Speed-walking in the hallway, my eyes settle on the last thing they'd have expected: Selena, alongside two men in suits.

She comes up to me and grabs my arms with both hands. "My God, Charles! That was intense!"

Before I can answer, one of the two suits interposes himself between us.

"Bob McIntyre, head of business at Warner." He hands me a business card and looks around to check whether anyone is looking.

The doors start opening, and Bob motions me to follow them. The other man starts talking as we all walk briskly away from the oncoming pack of people.

"We'd like to fly you in and have a sit down with you and some of our senior management," he says. "To make a long story short, we'd like to consider you to maybe head a large-scale venture our board recently approved. We think you'll be impressed."

"Were you guys even in there?" I say, catching my breath, every cell in my body pleading me to find a bed. "I'm not looking for any new projects. Besides, I've been flown to New York before. I know the script. Not interested." I look away from them and start walking faster toward the exit doors.

"Charles, please!" Selena pleads as she discreetly presses a business card into my hand. "At least listen to them!"

"I know you must be disappointed, Mr. Barca." Suit two demands the attention back. "We know what happened to you. Probably in more detail than even you do."

With that, he seizes my attention.

"But this is different," he says. "Trust us."

Chapter 13

"Numero uno," Andy says, cocking his index finger back. "If you want us to even have a chance here, you need to stop pissing streams of coke or whatever the heck it is you've been using."

He's sitting elevated behind his heavy oak desk, making him look a larger figure than he normally is. Ever the one to encourage life's little vices in a client, as it usually means an increased reliance on him, Andy's injunction to *just say no* actually resonates with me. When the greedy give selfless advice, one is compelled to listen.

"I'm being serious here, Charlie," he continues. "It's hard enough figuring out what the hell's going on ..." He pauses and shuffles the pile of documents on his desk between heavy breaths, "... *without* the client frying his brains and calling for friggin' Armageddon in public. The situation is serious, and I need more than half-a-Charles to deal with it. Okay?"

I half-a-Charles nod.

"Dos," he now holds up two fingers with gravity. "I don't know what took hold of you in Cannes, but you made a complete ass of yourself. My sources with two separate majors tell me you had a complete meltdown. MELT-DOWN," he stresses. "That's the exact word two different people used, independent of one another. Have you read the article in *Music Week*? Not very flattering. And the goddamn official MIDEM news wire picked up a Twitter feed from some young guy at Warner with a picture of you, captioned, "*I gave MDMA to that guy*! You can't keep putting us in these positions, Charles. You're better than this. You're sane. I mean, I think you're sane. For Christ's sake, Charles, I'm asking you to at least ACT sane, in public, for a few weeks. Okay?"

"First of all, Andy, your label sources are probably all in bed with PlayLouder or Universal one way or another. Tell them if *they* had any sense, they'd stop the tabloid gossiping, take my advice and jump off the Titanic. A-S-A-P."

"Not funny, Charles." He forces himself into a stern gaze. "I agreed to represent you, but not under conditions of self-sabotage. Don't be an asset, fine. But at least stop being such a friggin' *liability*, okay?"

I fake a yawn and look at my wrist, on which there is now no watch.

"I think some people actually liked my speech," I offer, in earnest. "If it makes you feel better, I almost didn't go through with it. But they insisted like crazy. So I said, fuck it."

"Fuck it?" He stares at me, up and down.

A healthy chuckle escapes me.

"Yes, actually," I answer. "That's *exactly* how it went down in my head, honest."

"Okay, whatever," he says, continuing to struggle with the spread of paper on his desk. "Beatrice!" he yells out. "Bring in the faxes from yesterday!"

"I don't think *everyone* thinks I'm crazy," I say. "Warner even wants to meet me, MDMA notwithstanding. At least according to this girl I met in Cannes. She's been all over me, trying to get me to visit her in New York."

Beatrice, a scruffy, middle-aged blond dressed in shades of brown, steps in and dumps yet more paper onto his desk.

"So, as I was saying," Andy continues, "I've heard a bunch of stuff, and I don't know what you actually said. But somehow it's true. For some out-there reason, Warner is going balls over you. They're eyeing you for this new start-up, fully funded by them and their online partners. They're talking executive package, stock options, everything. They want us in New York pronto, and I say we go ASAP. This may be the only head-high exit we have left."

"Well, if you *had* heard what I said," I say, "you'd know that I'm kind of done with the industry. Although I also don't want to accept PlayLouder *preventing* me to work in it for, what, four years?"

"Five."

"Well, five. I may change my mind at some point. Besides, if Warner were *that* serious, they'd know where to find me."

He sighs, extra audibly for effect. "You're not going to make this easy, are you?"

"Any news from PlayLouder?" I ask.

"So, Colin's lawyer calls me yesterday and says they'd up the offer by twenty-five percent if we add yet another year to the non-compete. I think there's more going on here than we thought. The goose is starting to lay golden, as they say! The buyout's the safest bet if you're serious about scramming for good. But Warner's the real jackpot if you want to dive into the industry and take the challenge head on."

I stay silent and mull this through.

"It all depends on you, Charles. Do you want to grow a beard and live in the Himalayas? You want a family? Wanna cut a rap album with Joaquin Phoenix? Or are you ready to step up and put your hot shot theories to the test? What do you really want? I can't answer those questions for you."

"Well, I think I did tell you where I was. I know I still want to make some kind of impact. I'd like to be able to help artists continue doing what they do, but outside this blood-sucking industry. Like this DJ girl I met in Cannes, Mini. Have you heard of her?"

"No," he says, looking at me severely.

"You should listen to her stuff. And you should see her, too. She's playing in Montreal at the end of the month. Maybe you could set something up with her management? We could...."

"Charles?"

"Yes?"

"We're on the cusp of the biggest opportunity of your life. You're seriously not going to get us sidetracked for some piece of tail, are you? It's like that Warner girl. You must get it that she's on you because of who you are, no?"

"And that would be?"

He looks at me in disbelief, making the doubt mount in me.

"You think so?" I say.

"Charles, Dennis Rodman couldn't get the rebound you're on right now. And you still have a lot of status from your industry days. For a girl, you're the perfect buy-low candidate. I smell it from miles away. You have to stay focused here."

"No, I know. It's just that...."

"Look, I hate to moralize. But you do need to grow up a little. You're not some freshman on a two-bit identity crisis. You're a business rock star. And somehow, you got a couple of big boys to come crawling at your feet." He looks at me with a pleading face now. "We're well positioned, but we can still fuck things up if you don't stop self-sabotaging. I'll drive the ship, just don't throw any rocks in it. And I'm serious. No more drugs. And no wild goose tail-chasing, at least for some time. And I need an answer, at least a general direction from you, soon. Can I count on you?"

I distantly nod.

Chapter 14

A few days into my new sobriety vow, and the only thing I've got to show for it is a freshly minted 3 a.m. wake-up routine: twenty minute bout of sweaty hypochondria, then a couple of hours of random web surfing, then exhausted fall back asleep and absurdly late midday wake-up. When lucky, as I am tonight, Selena's available for some gushy, long distance relationship-type chatting.

seljones: *guess what ... I'm visiting a friend in Montreal in 2 weeks - on the 20th!*
c.barca: *great ... can I ask u something?*
seljones: *J*
c.barca: *r ur bosses pressuring u to get close to me?*
seljones: *why u asking?*
c.barca: *r they?*
seljones: *well ... u do know they want u ... but they're not the only ones ;)*
c.barca: *is that a yes?*
(2 minutes of no answer)
c.barca: *hello?*

seljones: *what if I said so?*
c.barca: *r you?*
seljones: *no, but what would you think if I did?*
(Something along the lines of you being a conniving, careerist snake.)
c.barca: *Nothing. True?*
seljones: *well ... im sure they'd be glad if we did hook up ... but so would I ;)*

I close my laptop. Glacial gusts of wind are pounding my windows. I close my eyes and take in the lonely comfort of not having to be anyone for a few minutes. I re-open my computer, ignoring Selena's prompts. Mandy's new profile pic shows her, hair pulled back and wearing a tight tank top, with her beau waving his light brown dreadlocks like a shampoo commercial.

Selena sends me an SMS: *thinking of u... c u in mtl soon! xox*.

Ignore.

I go back to checking Mini's music online. No website, no Facebook, no MySpace, so I'm reduced to piecing a picture together from blogs, online articles, industry sources, German language interviews. Her last album sold in the low six figures worldwide, scored a few high-profile remixes, seems to be most popular in Australia and Northern Europe. I scour down her concerts page and find she's playing at Cherry, a club right up my street, on the same Friday that Selena is coming in. Reason enough to take out a calendar for the first time in months.

"Charlie! So glad you could make it!" Andy gets up and hugs me affectionately. It's 8:45 a.m. and we're at Lemeac, his favorite breakfast place.

"Kind of hard to ignore ten *urgent* SMS's coming in starting at seven am." I say, still forcing myself awake.

"Didn't I tell you it was important?" He ignores me and points to Nick and Clarice, who are sitting at the table with him.

"Nice to see you guys," I smile weakly, pushing back my frustration.

"Here's what's going on, Charles," Andy says, with way too much energy. "PlayLouder's making *big* mistakes. They've not so subtly told Nick and Clarice they might be next at the unemployment line very soon. They're targeting all those who were closest to you."

"It's true," Nick says, "they started putting the heat on me after I found out Mind Ventures and Universal were in bed from the start. Colin was in with them, too. He's turning the company into a goddamn software provider. My marketing staff is down to two. We both know what made this company, Charles. It was making the right bets on instinct, and...."

"Okay, slow down," I interrupt. "What do you mean, Universal and Mind were in bed from the start?"

"I intercepted a couple of e-mails. Universal indirectly funded the acquisition through Mind Ventures so they could use us as their digital arm. Everyone knew you'd never align with a major, and they were all foaming at the mouth to have first dibs on all our artists. Colin caught wind of the bidding war and aligned himself with the company that offered him the best succession plan. But here's the thing," Nick continues with excitement, as though in the middle of a rehearsed monologue, "the majority of our artists ended up refusing the offering. They preferred to stay independent. That's the big reason the company's been struggling since the acquisition. Of course, most of us in marketing knew that would happen. I'm sure you did too, but they didn't listen. Now they're talking about axing the whole division!"

My mind is impotently scouring through a dozen questions.

"Look, Nick, I'd shed a tear, I really would," I finally say. "But this is all alien talk to me right now. For all I care, they can take the whole thing for a joyride to hell and back."

"You're missing the point, Charlie," Andy interrupts. "And the point is this. Nick and Clarice are here to help us, to help *you*. Screw PlayLouder. Screw Universal. Screw them all, and screw their ridiculous plans. Don't you see this is why they've been increasing your buyout offers? Somehow, they know at least another major still has it hard for you. And Apple, Live Nation, Google, everyone else, they probably all do, too. Your market value is skyrocketing. But they're blue at the thought of you partnering with another major and putting a spotlight on their failures. That's why they're rushing to push you out of the industry pronto. Now, we can parlay all that interest and get the best deal out of Warner." He pauses and crosses his fingers in front of his face, beaming, turning his gaze to Nick and Clarice. "And when we do, you can get into your new Warner digs with your two most trusted soldiers by your side." He looks me on with a full face smile.

"It hasn't felt right since you left," Clarice says. "I mean, it's just been one mind game after another. First, no more coffee breaks. Then, the sick days. Then, they block my Facebook and personal e-mail on my work computer. I have to justify *every* single hour now. It's really terrible! I've had other opportunities, but I know what you can do. I'll even wait a few more weeks for you, if that's what it takes."

"Yeah, same here," Nick says. "I've been up for my annual raise since December, but not a single word from them to this day! I don't even know why I'm still there, to be honest."

"Charles, your mind's been running away from you," Andy continues, "because that's just how it works, right? But truth is you were never alone. We're all here for you. Right guys? Waitress!" He belts out, prompting the whole staff in the empty place to suddenly turn in our direction. "Can you get our friend here one of those caviar Benedict's and a latte?" He turns to me. "It's latte, right? Or cappuccino?"

I ignore him and turn to Nick and Clarice. "Look, I know you guys have nothing to do with what happened to me." They silently stare. "And I understand you're thinking about your careers. But the truth is my mind is not on any of this stuff right now. I'm trying to find something I can believe in again, something to be passionate about. To be honest, I don't see it coming from music, not while it's all such a goddamn mess."

Andy cuts in. "Charlie, Charlie, come on! Stop being such a downer! Opportunity is knocking! *Carpe Diem*! Only the strong survive! And you're the king of this jungle! Imagine how those guys are gonna feel when we stick it to them!"

His fists are clenched, and Nick and Clarice are staring on him with silently encouraging eyes.

"Look, we all know it's your move," he continues, "but you're too young, too talented to let opportunities like this slip by. So you've encountered a bump in the road. What great man hasn't? Even *I* failed a couple of bar exams, and I've poached *all* of my former employers' label clients. Except two, maybe." He's lost in thought for an instant. "But anyway! This is about you! And it's about the future of the whole goddamn music business. There's so much sense in all of this. Please tell me, tell *us* that you see it!"

I ponder this unusual order for a couple of seconds, six eyes voraciously tracking my every gesture.

"One thing's for sure," I finally say, eyes to myself. "I'm not diving into another situation that may end up a nightmare six years from now, just for the sake of some short term cash. Just not doing it." Their disappointment is tangible, and urges me to continue. "I never thought I'd become one of those whiney rich guys, moping about how fucked up their life is. But I can honestly say I've lost all the passion, all the meaning I thought I had in life. What happened to me was more than a bump in the road, Andy. And the weird part is, I'm starting to think maybe it was a road to bullshit. Maybe this is all a big blessing in disguise, although I can't figure out how, exactly, yet."

They're all puzzled, Clarice disoriented, even.

"Whatever carrot I was chasing," I say, "it couldn't have been *that* real, you know? Why else would I feel so empty right now? Where is everybody, everything I thought I was fighting and working for?"

Andy whispers to himself. He opens his mouth, but immediately draws his head back in, laying a concerned forehead on his closed fist. The thinking man with money on his mind.

"Look Charles," Nick butts in, "I understand you're putting things into question. But I have to take decisions in my own life, and I can't wait indefinitely. *You* understand that, right?"

"Yeah," Clarice adds, "I mean we do need to know, whatever you decide to do."

"I know," I say, as the waitress brings over my plate and a Cappuccino, or Latte. "I know you guys do."

Chapter 15

Cherry provides me with many elements that somehow hit me as home: good beats, an unsavory crowd, a graffitied back room where smoking is still tolerated, booths built deep into the walls to keep the vices private and the public wondering. It's one of the last remaining plays on the hedonistic haven that this city might have become had it not been for the rise of the government crony-corporatism of the Quebec nanny state. The club's barely been open for three months, and already inside word is that the corrupt zombies at the municipality are looking to revoke its alcohol license to have their insiders open a bar in an adjacent building. It's not that we don't believe in capitalism, in this last remaining French bastion of North America. It's that the government is every bit as voracious and self-serving as any private entity.

I've taken refuge in one of the booths, from where I now watch Selena walk in and look around. She's with a tall man in black-leather cowboy boots and a velvet blazer. She scans the room as he pays their cover. Before I can observe them some more, she spots me and quickly cuts toward me.

"So good to see you!" she says and gives me a tight hug, lifting herself off the floor. Her black tank top lifts up and I hold the bottom of her smooth, bare back. She smells of some naturally smelling perfume – lavender or lilacs, maybe.

"So who's the company?" I say in her ear.

She turns and pulls the man toward us.

"Charles, this is Paul Johnson. Paul, Charles."

"Hi, Charles, nice to meet you!" Paul extends his hand earnestly. I shake it, unable to suppress a mystified look at her.

"Paul's with our Toronto office," she explains. "Remember, I told you I was meeting up with a friend in Montreal?"

Indeed.

"So, are we getting drinks or what?" Paul says, as I lead them into my booth.

Four rounds later, I'm surprised that Paul and I are getting along like old buddies, while Selena's taken a seat on the outside looking in. The club's filling up quickly, and we've settled in my booth, basking anonymously in the sonic ambiance.

"So that's when we started signing new talent again," Paul says. "I doubt we'd do much artist development in Canada without the subsidies. The artists get to keep ownership of their stuff, we get rid of production hell. And we still keep most of the upside!"

"That's actually the only way we recommended that our artists hook up with a major," I say. "The days of glitz and glamour in front of the cameras and lifelong servitude behind them are over. And good riddance!"

"Indeed," he agrees, "and the market can only support so many Rihanna's at a time anyway. Look, Charles, I think you know that, as far as majors go, we're on the fast track to getting this digital thing down."

My quick glance at Selena finds her following us with the absent eyes of a spaced-out high school student. This doesn't stop Paul from continuing on emphatically.

"Just as a small example," he says, "thc online ad partnership we've just established with MTV is already sticking it to Universal-Sony's Vevo as the top online music destination. Over fifty million unique visitors every single month! You probably know that our parent company AOL-Time Warner is the one that funded Nullsoft, the company that created...."

"Gnutella." I cut in. "Yup, I know too well the long history of how you guys have ruthlessly backstabbed one another and the broader interest of the industry in search of the quick score."

"But it also means we've developed an expertise with decentralized technologies from the earliest stages." He doesn't skip a beat. "But these are all just interim steps in the big plan. We've yet to fully harvest the power of digital and go toward what we call deep digital integration. I was a huge fan of your speech, by the way, Charles. But you'd be surprised to find how far we are into that type of thinking already."

Paul and I go on for a bit, and we actually agree enough to bring me to a point of boredom. Meanwhile, we both pretend not to notice that Selena is shifting in and out of consciousness, thumbing away on her phone every few laboring moments. Paul shoots an annoyed stare at her, but she doesn't raise her head enough to even notice it.

"Anyway," Paul says, not concealing his irritation. "Want to join me for a smoke, Charles?"

"Sure." We get up, and I turn to Selena. "Do you wanna come with us?" I say.

"Uuh ... what?" she says. "No, no thanks. Got some work e-mails I need to get to."

Paul and I squeeze past the dance floor and, as we take the turn into the back room, I spot Mini setting up at the DJ booth.

"I'll be there in a minute." I tell Paul. I hesitate, and, just as my eyes cross her stare for an instant, I walk up to her.

"Hey there! Do you remember me?" I ask. "From Cannes?"

She looks up, and seems to recognize me only after a few awkward seconds. "Yes, I think so," she says, then looks back down toward her gear. "You're the guy who gave that crazy speech, no?" She pauses, thinks to herself. "We also met on the bus, no?"

"Really? I'm not sure, I don't...." I hesitate, realizing now that there is no other place from which she *could* recognize me. Quite the feeling, getting caught in one's self-spun web of hogshit. She smiles to herself, as though to insinuate that we both know better, then goes back to her computer.

"So," I shake that off, "your boyfriend isn't here with you?"

"Who, Lothar? No, I left him at home with the kids."

I nod and hold my breath.

"I'm joking," she says. "He's just my manager. Was my manager. Whatever."

"Sounds like your stuff is really together," I say.

"Look who's talking!" she says, looking up and pushes my shoulder affectionately, I think. I hope.

"Sorry to interrupt!" Paul says, and he angles between us, smiling at Mini. "Care to join us for a smoke?" he asks her.

She looks at me, surprised. "Umm, no, thank you. I still need to set up."

"I'll be right there, Paul," I say, slanting my body so as to squeeze him out.

"Look," I say, leaning in, "maybe this isn't the best time or place...." This kind of nervousness has eluded me for years, my usual targets tending to be of the mentally-challenged model variety; definitely not the kind whose talents I genuinely respect. "I've heard your music ... I ... can we be in touch somehow?"

She hesitates. "Okay," she says, "leave me your e-mail." The smoother the rejection the more bitter the sting, I'm thinking. Nevertheless, I write my e-mail down on a napkin and hand it to her.

She gives me a faint, parting smile, and turns back to her screen.

"We're not hiding it," Paul says, more serious and resolute now. "You're hands down the number one target here."

We're back at the booth with Selena, and he's slowly wearing me out, shifting gears, from personal talk back to business, back and forth, inexhaustible. Mini's set is halfway in, but I can barely make out any sounds from her music, as Paul is working to keep his face square in front of mine.

"I mean, who better to spearhead something like this?" he continues. "Tell me, who? We're on the cusp of the next great music revolution, and we think you're the guy to put it all together for us." I take another glance toward Selena, but she's still tapping and frowning.

"We don't want to pressure you," Paul continues, "but we do need to make some decisions quickly. Give us a chance to show you what we're working on. Actually, some of our key guys from New York happen to be in town. Think about it. Wait ... just wait for me here, okay? I'll be right back," he says, and darts out.

"Okay, Charles?" Selena says, pumping a few final characters into her phone before turning to me.

"Yes?"

"I wanna go," she says.

"What?"

"I wanna go!" she repeats in a whine. "Are you bringing me or not?"

"What? Bring you? Where? Aren't you here with ..."

"You don't think I see through your little game? I saw you giving your number to that girl!"

I pause, as I experience a sudden feeling of guilt I don't feel I deserve.

"And pretending to be all like best friends with Paul!" she continues. "Please! You think I came all the way here so you could treat me like *shit*?"

"Are you being serious?" I say, but she just looks at me with an empty stare. "You brought one of your bosses over, for God's sake. And you get mad at me because I actually get along with him?"

"Whatever," she says, drawing back to her phone.

"Selena," I grab her hand as she refuses to look up to me, "I don't get it, I...."

"I know you don't get it, Charles!" She looks up, face red and furious. "That's the point, you don't get it! I mean, to you, I'm probably just another groupie in that bullshit rock-star life of yours, right?" She stares me down with the penetrating gaze of someone clearly prepped for war. "What happened in Cannes meant something to me. And you don't understand the pressure they've been putting on me! I mean, I just can't lose my job! Not with this stupid recession, not with all my loans. And I thought ... I don't know!"

"What? You thought what?"

"I thought we had something real! Don't even say it, I know. I'm a big fool."

"Hey ... don't say that ..." I say, trying to quell her feelings. "I.... we did have a good time in Cannes...." I stumble, realizing I'm on slippery, unrehearsed terrain in front of someone whose ideas are much more together than mine. "There's no problem in us being friends and seeing where things go, is there?" I feel a pitiable pride at having said something that sounds virtuous and half-coherent.

"Friends! Ha! Yeah, cool, let's be friends," she says, sourly, and puts her head down. Then, suddenly, she launches herself at me, full body, and engages my mouth frantically, making small, grunting sounds as her tongue and lips attack mine, her moist, teary cheek rubbing all over my face. A sense of dread clutches me. I pull back and find her, completely red-faced, looking at me with pleading eyes.

"What's wrong with you?" she says, her tone not aggressive as much as haunting this time.

"Nothing's *wrong* Selena, I just ... don't want to give you any false hopes at this point, I guess."

"Wow, so you really *don't* give a damn." She snaps back, waiting for me to answer, which I don't. "You don't, eh? Figures. That's who I always fall for. The type who doesn't give a fuck."

"That's not true," I say. "I mean, I do care, I guess, it's just...."

"You care, just not that much."

I realize she may actually be right, but admitting so would be catastrophic, so I decide to just shut up.

"Whatever," she continues in disappointment, almost to herself, but still loud enough for me to hear. "I'm thinking of the next twenty years of my life, I want to fall in love with someone, and making myself available like that. And you're being such a total insensitive prick about it."

"How *could* you be in love with me?" I finally say, caving in to a rising indignation. "You barely know me! We met for one night in Cannes, where you basically ran on me! Why *would* you be in love? Because you listened to your bosses and Googled the shit out of me and figured it was a good time to buy low on a good long term prospect? It's suspect. I'm sorry, Selena, but your idea of love is fucking suspect. I don't want that kind of love in my life anymore. It's selfish love. If you love me, that word is absolutely bankrupt. It means zero, nothing."

"You're an asshole!" she yells and thwacks my left cheek and ear with a full hand. "You're such a big fucking asshole!"

I stare at her in disbelief, as Paul gets back to the booth a few seconds later.

"Hey guys!" he says, scanning us quickly. "Everything alright here?"

"Yeah," I say, as Selena slips under his stare like an old pro. "Everything's just perfect."

"You're not making our star feel uncomfortable, are you, Selena?" Paul says, in a tone sound both joking and menacing.

"Of course not, Paul!" she says, and for the first time glances at him flirtatiously.

"Well," I say, suddenly feeling a lack of oxygen and an urgent need to be free from these two, "I've heard enough good stuff tonight. How about that meeting tomorrow, Paul?" I grab his shoulder, get up and start walking out. "Can that can be arranged?" I hand him one of Andy's business cards. "We can meet at my lawyer's office, early afternoon."

"Of course!" He snatches the card and places it carefully into his wallet. "I mean, that's why we all met tonight, after all, isn't it?"

"Yup," I say, catching Selena's eyes briefly. "It sure is."

Paul and Selena at bay, I go back into the club, where the crowd is quickly thinning out. I swim against the current of people heading to the door and spot Mini, alone at the bar, sipping a yellow drink, legs crossed, eyes to herself. I now realize I've missed her entire set.

"Never too late for a drink for you Germans, is it?" I say, smiling at her, hoping to prompt one in return.

"For pineapple juice, no," she answers, plainly.

"Pineapple juice?"

"It's good," she looks away. I'd noticed her features before, but this close up they're even more fascinating. Her limbs are long and delicate, her flesh alive, smooth stretches of white skin punctuated by perky beauty marks. Once you push through the large tattoos and tribal earrings and lanky orange t-shirt, the reward is a place where everything is where nature intended it to be.

"Can I have one of those?" I motion to the bartender – skinny, soulless model-type with loud makeup.

"Sorry, last call was ten minutes ago," she answers, swiping the bar aggressively with a wet cloth.

"Even for pineapple juice?" She looks at me like I've just broken some kind of spell and briskly scoots to the mini fridge to pour me one.

Mini laughs to herself discreetly, then turns toward me. "So, you liked the set?" she asks. "It's a new style I'm playing with."

"Umm ... yeah. Yeah, it's a great style."

"You didn't even hear it," she says, locking my eyes in now and not letting me look away.

"How do you know?" I chuckle.

"I saw you talking with those two people the whole time. Why do you lie?"

"I ... I don't know," I say, unable to bluff this time.

"I know you are the guy we met on the bus. You lied about not being that big web company guy or whatever. It was pretty funny. You put Lothar in his place. It's rare that I see that."

I'm thankful for her remembering at least some details about me, but I still can't decide whether she's mocking or complimenting me.

"You're right, I guess," I answer. "Look, in Cannes, I just didn't want to have anything to do with the business anymore. I wanted to be someone else for a few days. Your career looks like fun and everything, but trust me, the other side is uglier than you think. It's killed my love for music. Look at tonight. You're an artist I genuinely like, and I can't even listen, because my blood is being sucked by two corporate lechers all night."

She bends her head slightly, in approval, I hope.

"Anyway," I continue, "I'm pretty sure it's all over now. I'm pulling the plug on everything. Tomorrow's probably my last two hours in this goddamn business."

"Your heart is not right," she says, too casually to put me on the defensive. "You say you love music, but you only hold on to what you hate about it."

I can't find words to answer coherently.

"You see for me," she says, looking up, "I'm really finished with it." Her moves are gracious and solid, deeply centered somehow, as though stemming from a large tree. "I'm leaving and not telling anyone. My management, my label, my publisher, my contracts, whatever, they are all gone in my head. I'm going to make real music again, alone." Her face and body get closer to mine. "I *need* to make it because I love it. Doing something is only a choice if you don't really love the thing itself."

"Well, I hope you continue doing the stuff you're doing. I really like...."

"I won't. It's not me anymore. It's too produced, too indirect. It's not transcribing the movements of my soul. It's more of this," she points to a small mandolin next to her DJ equipment. "With electro, my technology was always improving, the label got me more technical producers all the time. But *I* stopped improving. I wish I could be like those jazz players from the twenties, playing with the same old sax every night for thirty years. The only way to improve the music was to improve *yourself*."

She's speaking with her hands now, emotion flowing from her in a way I haven't seen before.

"With music you could overcome your limitations, give more of yourself, become something greater. Today, technology gives almost everything. There's less room for the human transformation."

If her intention was to make me feel idiotic, she hit the mark dead on. "Look, obviously I'm no musician," I say, "but I think that applies to other things, too."

She nods laconically. I'm irresistibly drawn to her. I consider asking her where she's staying for the night, ask if I can help her somehow. But something about her doesn't let me go there; some purity I can't explain.

"You don't have to be a musician," she says. "It's just a channel. You sound sick about a lot of things. Your pain is because you still think they are useful to you. Tell me, if you decided to leave everything, just leave all your old self behind, would you be allowed to do it? Or would you find some excuses to stay attached to your misery?"

"Leave? Of course I could. In fact, I have. Three times in the last couple of months, actually."

"But you're back in the same place."

"Yeah but ... Look, one thing I *will* say about my life, I can do whatever the hell I want. No one can stop me, trust me. I can go *anywhere*, but how will that help me with anything? I still have the reality of my life to deal with. I still have to decide what it is I really want."

"It's not where but also how." She holds my eyes again.

"Okay, look, I'm good." I look away, irritated, as I sense we're veering into a vague, wishy-washy zone where words stop having real meaning. "Why," I turn back to her, "are *you* going anywhere?"

"Somewhere music still gives people the right emotions, not just status or pride." She looks into her glass, as though the answer were contained in it. "Somewhere slow. Maybe with some plants. And small animals."

"Plants and animals? You?" I say. "Please. You seem like you'd be lost without your urban subcultures and after-hours."

She grins. "What, because of this?" She points to a poem tattoo on her long, delicate neck. "I'm from a normal family in a small Bavarian town. I like a slow, peaceful life."

"Please," I give her a sceptical stare, but am unable to come up with anything else.

"Anyway, we're talking in the air. I'm leaving, and you're going back to an office building to talk to people you hate about things that depress you. Good luck," she says, and starts getting up.

"So you still don't think I could leave?" I say. She smiles delicately and turns toward her gear.

I reach out and grasp her arm. "Mini, look, life just passes and we could just never see each other again. I want us to stay in touch somehow."

"Okay," she says, but not reacting.

"Give me your phone."

"Why?"

"Just give it."

She hands me her iPhone and I type in my e-mail myself.

"Please, use it," I say.

She nods and goes back to packing her stuff.

Chapter 16

"So let's assume we accept that those stock options only start kicking in after year one," Andy roars as the three-headed Warner monster watches on attentively. Selena's also there, sipping her coffee, legs crossed.

"I'm not saying we do accept it," Andy continues. "But *if* we do, at some hypothetical point in the future, it'll be because you'd given us a much larger signing bonus."

Two p.m., my eyes are puffy, my mouth is dry and still tastes of pineapple. I consider jumping in to ask if I can have a few more days, weeks, months, before we get gritty with detail, but the energy in the room is too high and mine too low for anything to be done.

"Well, we'd have to discuss that internally," one of them says, "but we're open to the idea. Control is more important to us than cash at this stage."

"Yeah," Selena interjects, "I think we need to see that Charles can show some commitment."

I look at her in puzzlement.

"Look," Paul butts in, "we'll work something out, guys. Charles will get top treatment. Let's not get too bogged down over the details."

"Agreed," Andy says, game face screwed on tightly. "Let's keep the big picture in mind."

I surf down to Yahoo News. Apparently, an airport in Mongolia was shut down because of a UFO sighting.

"Moving on," Andy continues, "what about Charles' team? He has two key PlayLouder employees willing to join him from day one."

"We don't have a problem with that," says the third guy, Bob or Brian or Bill, my future "liaison" at Warner, the guy I would "report" to, "when" I integrate the happy family. "But first we need to get to one of our main concerns. There's a perception out there, right or wrong, that there are ... how shall I say this, that Mr. Barca may have had some *character* issues in the past. Now, between us, it's nothing we haven't seen before. But some of our white-haired folks have expressed some concern about his sometimes brash behavior. They want us to work in some airtight good behavior clauses in any agreement."

"Tell'em that's why I succeed," I say, in my first words of the day. "Because I go places no board member white-haired folks have gone before."

"Charles!" Andy says.

"It's one thing to be a bit of a maverick," B-guy snaps back at me. "But it's quite another to be linked to drugs and call out for mass crimes in public, isn't it?"

"Did you really just go there?" Andy says, turning to the others. "Paul, did he just go there? I clearly said before we came in here, NO blackmailing about Cannes. And here we are, talking about Cannes! Actually, while we're on the topic, let me just say this. If it weren't for Charles' little performance out there – irritating as it may have been to some – we probably wouldn't be sitting here right now!"

"Guys," Paul says, turning to his two guys, "we're losing sight here. Maybe we'll do an ironic press conference or something, poke some fun at the situation. I mean, people have short memories nowadays, right?"

"Fine, but we still have to agree on some wording," B-man cuts in before I can respond. "You know we're a public company now, and we're run like one. Important people are nervous. That's a fact. We may as well be honest and get that out of the way."

The other guy, from their legal team, nods somberly from across the table.

"So?" Andy says. "Is it?"

"What?" Paul says.

"Out of the way! Is it out of the way!" Andy says. "Are we here to make a deal or to crucify Charles for stating his opinions, which are highly educated, expert opinions by the way!"

"Mr. McDonough," B-man turns to Andy, "we don't want you getting the wrong idea. We're only being upfront because we're willing to commit significant resources here. This will define the nature of the music market for the next generation. We need Charles to understand there's a big picture here."

"We hear you," Andy retorts. "We're definitely here to make a deal, too. So we'll listen to you. Right, Charles? We can hear them?"

I nod.

"Well," B. continues, "as I said, with the physical market being what it is, it's possible this division will eventually run the whole label one day...."

And so the chatter rolls on. I scroll down my iPhone to watch messages come in real time. My heart almost skips when an e-mail from Mini suddenly pops up: *if u can really, maybe we'll meet in Ipanema?* No "xo" or flirtatious signatures, but still, a lifeboat, a ray of hope, a sign for my tired mind to latch on to. I can't help but smile, but then Selena catches my stare and forces me into a serious sulk again. The others are so absorbed in the discussion they don't notice a thing.

"No, yes, we fully realize this. We do." Andy says, in response to I'm not sure what. "Listen, at the end of the day we are firmly dedicated to this deal. Completely."

"I think Charles also has to show that he can be loyal, too," Selena bumps in.

I look up to her again, perplexed. She squints down toward a blank sheet of paper and starts doodling.

"Well, naturally," B-guy says, "there would be standard non-competes across the board, if that's what you meant, Selena."

She nods in approval.

"Sure, we understand," Andy says. "All that standard stuff, no problem. So in an ideal world, when and how would everything get started?"

"Probably with a two-week red carpet orientation in New York," Paul answers. "Maybe in a couple of weeks."

A couple of weeks?

"Then the plan was to have a twelve month kick-start at the Toronto office before the show moves to New York full-time. The kinks have to be ironed out before we bring this into head office."

"Not doing Toronto for a year." I say. They all turn to me with baffled stares. "Andy, can I talk to you alone for a minute?"

"Wha.... Yes, of course," he says. "We'll just be a minute, guys. You want something to drink?" They all nod no. "Beatrice!" he yells out, and she rushes right in. "Get these gentlemen some drinks please!"

Andy and I walk into his office. He shuts the door, doesn't sit.

"What the hell is going on, Charles?" he says.

"Isn't it a bit early to talk about friggin' orientations? I haven't decided anything yet, and PlayLouder...."

"Don't tell me you're still thinking about fucking PlayLouder! Warner's about to put you on a global pedestal! You'll be a prince of industry! You'll easily make five times as much as the PlayLouder buyout with Warner over the next two to three years, which means more money for all of us...."

"Andy," I stop him. "You are not listening to me! I don't even *want* a fucking job right now! Do you get that?"

He stares at me severely.

"I want to figure out what I really want in life before I make any big decisions. And I haven't really coming up with any great answers yet. Are you following any of this?"

He swings his arms in frustration. "Charles, you have to understand! This opportunity will vanish just as fast as it appeared. It's golden!"

"I know ... on paper. But life isn't on paper. I'm sorry. I can't pretend to be somewhere I'm not."

"Okay, listen up," he says, his complete lack of hesitation making me wonder whether he's even considered what I've said.

"Let's go back in there and get a firm offer. Then, we'll sit down and talk about what you want to do. I promise you, whatever that is, WHATEVER you want, if it's to open a small vinyl shop on a Caribbean island, or start a new-age cult in Nepal, I will help you achieve it better if we have that offer in hand. Deal?"

Even as my body demands that I fire the prick on the spot, the bit of reason he's hit me with strikes me as irresistible.

"Okay," I finally say.

We walk back into the conference room, and Andy claps his hands as he grabs his chair and sits. "Sorry 'bout that, gents," he says. "Charles just never had it big for Toronto. SO, where were we? Ah yes, the golden parachute. Or at least, its less intimidating younger brother, the silver life vest!"

Everyone in the room laughs politely, as though some deep, insightful inside joke had just been cracked. I feel the onset of nausea.

"Before we move on to that," Bill-Bob says, "let me just stress that we have a new and strict drug-free policy with all of our executives. The last thing we want is a Sean Parker situation on our hands."

"No need to worry about that!" Andy says. "Charles earned his party-boy rep in the early days of PlayLouder. What you have in front of you now is a mature man, ready for the responsibilities of success. He'll walk right through any test you can put in front of him. Right, Charles?"

I nod pensively, thoughts flowing to Mini.

"Also," Paul says, "we don't want to put any pressure on Charles, and we're not saying we need an answer right today, but...."

"Time is most definitely of the essence here," Andy says. "We completely agree, and we're committed to making a move soon, too."

"Exactly," Paul answers. "I mean, you know how rapid-fire the field is, and we'd like to know what the major pieces are before rolling out our plans and strategies for the next year. I was even thinking, if we're all committed to this, we can even start having the preliminary meetings next week even if the ink hasn't dried yet." Andy nods and starts opening his mouth to talk when I interrupt him.

"Can't do next week," I say.

"Why not?" Andy asks.

All eyes turn and lock in on me simultaneously.

"I'll be out of town."

Chapter 17

Life on Rio's Vinicius De Moraes Avenue trickles forth to the steady drip of a lazy morning sun. Passers-by push forward on the earth-incrusted cobblestones, carrying odd items, like old leather pouches or water-wrinkled notepads, infused by what strikes me as an unmistakably *foreign* sense of zest. Palm trees and large, looping plants burst out of the earth unevenly, revealing no discernible pattern, stretching out like nonchalant tentacles across and over rusty magazine stands, old record stores, and a slew of general, nondescript locales where you can get anything from breakfast to your muffler repaired.

A ten-year old boy in a *2008 Lakers NBA Champion* T-shirt and flip-flops three sizes too big waves me in and impels me, "Um poquo dinheiro! Poh favoh, playboy!", outstretching his hand in earnest.

"Playboy?" I whisper to myself pensively, wondering whether I've lost my marbles or if the Celtics hadn't actually won the championship that year.

He rolls his eyes and gestures me off as one might do to an insignificant insect.

I walk into what has become my sanctuary in Rio – a large, modern, air conditioned bookstore called *Lettras Y espressoes*, where 24/7 Wi-Fi access and an English magazine stand give me a much needed daily dose of calm. I settle in front of my laptop, next to a few quiet Brazilians who, disappointingly, look rather like healthier versions of myself than the transcendental Carnaval hedonists I've seen on television. Three days of walking up and down the twisting boardwalk, of reading Mini's e-mail, wondering why she hasn't answered my two attempts to reach her yet, of eating churros and feeling the fat cells multiply and get cosier next to one another; three days of checking my phone and inbox obsessively, re-reading Mini's e-mail again and again, trying to decrypt hidden messages in it, searching for the redemptory clue in so much vain. Nothing to show for going on three days but tired eyes and a mind on neutral. I sigh and take in the soothing, reliably available breeze of modernity and continue surfing. World news, miscellaneous stories, sports updates, Wayne Gretzky's slutty daughter on TM fucking Z. I wish that the Internet were more like television, that I wasn't in charge of the programming all the time. That the show was determined by someone, something, other than myself. Nope. I'm terminally locked within the patterns of my own ridiculously predictable mind. *Lettras* does, however, offer a cure against the recurring irritants of this place: the ever-present humidity, the wild, encroaching flora, the scorching tropical sun, the panhandling favela kids, the unrecognizable smells, the old, leather-skinned troubadours on the steps of decrepit apartment buildings.

Any number of things that appear so harmless and folkloric at first but quickly oppress one as too intense, too persistent, when experienced in real life. That's how it all feels to me this morning, anyway. Nothing too inspiring.

"You take a right," said Alain, a slender French man in his forties, pointing to our street corner, on the day I arrived to Rio, "Eets ze beach. You go left, fifty meters. It's dangerous Favela."

I've shacked up at *Casa 6*, a small bed and breakfast in Ipanema run by Alain. His precise movements and drooping brown eyes suggest unspoken personal dramas he probably fled in coming to live in Rio. Or maybe that's in my head.

Still, he's proving to be a friendly and reliable guide through the security maze of this supposedly "laid back" city. At the same time, he spares no energy convincing me that Cariocas are "the friendliest people on earth," and that trouble tends to stay away as long as one lives by a small number of cardinal security rules: number one, "in Rio, fashion kills." No Diesel print T-shirts, no Dolce Gabbana glasses. No fake Rolex watches or ripped jeans or cute Billabong surfer shorts. "It's really class warfare here," he told me. "Wearing fashion things, this is provocation for them." Also, no beach after seven p.m., when the friendly soccer kids reportedly turn into blood-thirsty Gremlin monsters, and one should jump into a taxi and head home promptly. "Look, it's not Canada; it's not France," he said. "But I'm here twenty years, and I'm still alive!" The pride he exuded when saying this did not make me feel any safer.

Not sure why, but I can't manage to stretch my morning walks on the beach any longer than twenty minutes at a time. Then, greasy croissant and latté at one of the many Parisian-style cafés. Then, on to *Lettras*, where online Charleswatch has reached fever pitch. PlayLouder's having Clarice send me a slew of new lawyers' letters. The latest is a five-pager, where they manage to both increase the buy-out sum and threaten to rip my life to shreds if I don't answer on time. The function of legalese: to mask the idiocy of executive decisions with the language of rationality.

On the Facebook front, Mandy's mobile updates are now a daily occurrence. One of the emerging mysteries in my life: if I have no feelings left for her – which I most definitely don't – why do I spend such an inordinate amount of time picking her life apart? To her credit, she *is* the queen of harmless vanity entertainment. Yesterday saw her launch a new group called *Free Yoga for the Impoverished.* The wretched of the earth will now be adorned with rounder asses and better posture. There may be hope for world social justice after all.

Selena is seeking solace from me, and I find a modicum of comfort in knowing that someone seems to care, even if in a completely self-interested way, about me. *"Good time we had in mtl"*, she tells me. *"... had way too much to drink tho ;) NE way ... hope things r good wit u ... c u in NYC soon? xoxox.*

Roland Barthes said it best: "I speak, and you hear me, therefore *we* exist."

I find myself wondering what life would be like with Selena in New York. Big lofts, long days, tall buildings, dizzy nights, rich friends, trendy clubs. All things considered, life on earth *could* be a lot worse, I suppose.

Back at *Casa 6*, I'm moderately comforted at seeing the faces of the guests, most of whom have now become familiar enough that we can exchange cordial, muffled salutes. They're typically young, European, educated, curious. To me, the whole setting is a rather average play on the "colourful international bunch," the *Auberge Espagnole* "we're all different but really all the same" brand of bland Erasmus pop internationalism.

I gather, from the disjointed bits of conversation, that most have already been to Brazil. They can exchange basic Portuguese greetings – "Tudo Legao!" ... "Mutu tranquilo!" – and tips on dancing Capoeira and Forro. When they come back from the clubs in Lappa or the local Ipanema bars, their late nights are capped with sophomoric discussions on the state of the world/solar system/universe. The accepted oracle of wisdom here is Chela, a bearded Spanish Eastern Philosophy professor. His job description, long blond mane, white attire and soft voice all properly credential him for the role he plays with the others. It also doesn't hurt that he's the official pot supplier in the Casa. Somehow, through the operation of some modern semiological magic trick, it all amounts to giving him the last word in all conversations, the key insight always delivered in a slow, dreamy drawl, the thick Spanish accent only adding suspense to the glorious reception of truth by the others. Some quizzical and entirely indeterminate statement like, "be one with all" or "lose your attachments" will punctuate hours of joint-smoking and story-telling about the latest sexual conquest of so and so, or the most recent rumour from the vicious favela wars.

I've learned to suppress my many, "Yeah, but," moments, refusing to play the part of the disillusioned urban cynic who spoils everyone's fun by injecting a dose of reality – that disintegrating, venomous poison – onto words that seem, on the face of it, anyway, to have an uplifting effect on everyone.

Chela also adheres to a strict policy of chastity within the bed and breakfast, and, as far as I can tell, outside of it as well. According to him, pop culture is responsible for our obsession with sex, and the sexual impulse is "selfish at bottom, and only brings pain in the long term." Having adopted the role of de facto leader, and taking it with the minimum of integrity it requires, he's made it a point to integrate me into the group discussions, which I've been ably deflecting. Antoine and Françoise, the Parisians, are the only two with whom I've had more than passing conversations. Theirs is one of those friendships with clearly unresolved sexual tension. His playful ribbings and her amused rejections are normally followed by grand social theorizing by both. I wish I could help the guy out, let him know that his strategy of seeking to get laid by quoting Zen monks and bearded socialists is a rather flawed one from the start, but I can't muster enough force to ever actually do it. For the most part, I realize I may have unconsciously internalized Chela's path of resignation: observing everything, taking part in nothing, waiting for Mini, waiting for answers, swallowing the dour pill of existence as calmly and painlessly as I can possibly muster.

Alone in my room now, as the chatter rumbles on in the living room downstairs, the browsing gods take me to Obama, Osama, and all the BS in between. I'm briefly disturbed by my general indifference toward those abstract happenings that most people consider to be the "major events in the world."

Then, I browse to Air Canada's site and look up some possible return flights, which feels reassuring, as it convinces me I haven't completely lost my mind.

Chapter 18

At Antoine's insistence, I forego this morning's Internet session and finally accept to follow him at one of those beach soccer matches.

"When in Rome you must train with the gladiators, no?"

I'm exhausted already. One last excuse creaks into being. "But I have no soccer shoes."

Antoine looks at me as though I've spoken an alien tongue. "This is a soccer match on Copacabana beach, not the World Cup. No one has shoes."

We arrive at the beach mid-afternoon to a dozen guys skilling around with soccer balls. Without a word being spoken, the teams automatically divide into two: Europeans on one side, Brazilians on the other.

"You can have the Canadian!" Antoine jokes to the Brazilians. They immediately welcome me with smiles and politely gesture for me to take one of the striker spots. Then, the game starts.

I've watched just about enough soccer in my life to notice the clash of styles between Euro football and Brazilian *futebol.* I'd always assumed it was a clash between order and chaos, between following rigid rules on one hand and free improvisation on the other. Following their game from the inside, though, I now realize that Brazilians do have patterns of their own. The difference is, rather, in the motivation: enjoyment *during* the game seems as valuable to them as victory after it.

More importantly, they're so skilled that they manage to have me score a couple of easy goals, of the tap-in variety. On those rare occasions where the play requires that I actually do something with the ball mid-flow, everything pauses and can only restart once I get rid of it. I'm the recurring bastard note in a great symphony.

We win the first game 10-3, and I finally gasp for air. I peel off my T-shirt like a layer of soaked, exhausted skin.

"No more!" I wave to my teammates and inch toward the sidelines, expecting an equal amount of relief on their part.

But they refuse my request, and instead insist for me to stay on. "Vem! Vem!" they say insistently, pointing toward the goalie, who seems excited to get to play forward. He slaps me five with joy, compelling me to accept the offer.

My limbs move mechanically into goalie position, and game two begins. I immediately make a couple of big, lucky saves, and the encouragement from my teammates fills me with excitement. Meanwhile, my team strings together three quick goals. Then, still basking in my new-found pride ("*maybe I just needed to find my position*") I let in two easy goals in succession. The teams go back and forth in what has now become an unexpectedly competitive match. The sun is roasting my shoulders and face into a bright red, but my T-shirt is soaked and full of sand, and I can't put it back on. Suddenly, the score is 9-8 for the Europeans, and eating one more goal would mean an unthinkable loss for the Carioca All-stars. While the action is on the other side, I hunch down in pain, hands on knees, the sun pressing down on me without mercy, and swipe the salty sweat from my face, urging myself to hang in there. I open and close my eyes a few times to regain my focus, and my stare converges on the stuffed roll of white flab that now passes as my midsection. I experience it almost as an explanation – a panoramic, split-second recall of expensive dinners, binge cocktailing and self-indulgence. A lipidic symbol of my voracity.

Before I fully grasp the idea, I snap back into the game to screams from my teammates. "A bola! A bola!" I panic, and, when I see them pointing upward, I look and see the ball arcing up toward the sky. I hone in on it, legs cocking slowly as I prepare to jump, eager for my chance to repay the Brazilians for being so forgiving of my incompetence, my chance to finally justify my presence in this game. I lower my eyes and see a guy from the other team, a trash-talking bully of a Brit, making a run toward me full steam, gearing up for a header.

I might be the dumb Canadian, but I do remember goalies can use hands to catch the ball mid-air. I size up the Brit quickly and turn my gaze back to the ball, clenching my fists. My eyes get bigger, lips tighten, breathing stops. The ball starts speeding down toward us, and the Brit springs down for a jump. In what feels like an exaggerated, slow-motion moment, my feet push off the sand and I thrust myself upward, in a kind of awkward Superman pose. I see the Brit jumping as well, angling to hit the ball with his head. And, just as we apex in mid-air together, we collide violently. My clenched fist first whacks his teeth and nose, then my shoulder crashes down on his face as we fall down. A pop ensues, then a crack.

"Aaaaargh!! Fuck!! What the fuck!" he screams, springing to his feet and towering over me. A generous gush of blood splashes down from his face onto me. I squeeze away from him, but he tackles me back down and starts swinging madly.

"Fuuuuuck!!" He yells, squirting and squealing like a hog at the slaughterhouse, his blood oozing all over me like warm tanning oil. I cover up as best I can and only see glimpses of his face. His eyes are overtaken by fury, and he grabs my neck now, sinking his nails into my flesh, sending knuckles pounding against any part of my body he can catch.

I grab his wrists instinctively and, somehow, manage to swivel him onto his back. I get up and hop away from him.

"Relax!!" I yell at him, knees buckling, my arms and face now covered with a thick paste of blood and sand. I feel as though any gust of wind would blow me over.

Then, suddenly, four Brazilians hop in front of the Brit. Three of them take him down by the shoulders, as softly as a raving maniac can possibly be taken down. The other one pushes me a few steps away from the action.

"Helax, man, helax," he tells me.

The Europeans are converged a few meters away, looking outraged, debriefing at safe distance. A couple of them slowly move toward the Brit, trying to calm him down. "I'll fuckin' kill that fuckin' wanker!" he screams, over and over.

"Come on man," Antoine says, pulling me away. "Let's get out of here. Obrigado."

I wish I could thank the Brazilians too, but my head is all mush. I grab my T-shirt, thick filets of blood streaming visibly from my right arm, and we start walking briskly along the beach, back toward Ipanema.

"How amazing was that!" Antoine exclaims.

"Not very," I whisper to myself, as I wash up in the salt water, trying to figure out where all my cuts and welts are. My mind hasn't settled enough to make sentences yet, but my heart rate has slowed some. The water is peaceful and full, and the lowering sun pushes down slightly on my sunburnt skin. I'm still trembling, but the action already feels like miles away.

"Did you see how quickly they took control?" Antoine continues, in excitement. "It's amazing!"

The warm breeze envelops me in a comforting air and I feel no urge to respond.

"These guys would kill you for fifty bucks at one a.m. But on their beach, it's their time, their moment for fun. No violence allowed!"

I usually enjoy Antoine's harmless philosophical banter, but, for once, I wish he'd just shut up. Instead, he figures my silence means he's on an unstoppable roll.

"In the West, murder is either political or psychological, you know? No one really understands why it happens. Sometimes it's done by society and justified by the experts. Sometimes, it's because someone is crazy and it's just psycho stuff. But here, it's completely logical. It's because society pretends these kids don't exist and they have fucking nothing. It's a real, social violence. But it never gets in the way of fun. No way. The only thing sacred is fun. It's because every day can be the last. They are forced to live in the moment. The fun and the violence, they are together, and they make sense, you know?"

I think back to the stories of dismembered journalists and kamikaze favela kids peppering bullets on random people, but don't engage. "I hear you," is all I can offer, as we hear the victorious chants of "ACAI!" from a nearby vendor.

"Come on! Here," Antoine says, as he tends a few Reals to the guy, grabs a couple of small, purple slush plastic cups and tends one to me. "This is the healthiest snack on the planet, man. I was here a few years ago and it was the exact same guy selling it! Way before an American entrepreneur turned it into supposedly a big discovery and a billion dollar business. Now they sell Acai pills for weight loss and erectile dysfunction. Whatever!"

I ignore him and plunge the cold, grainy pulp into my mouth, letting it melt, slowly and painfully, against my palate. My face is full of emerging bruises and small cuts, and the salt water makes me feel each one of them distinctly. But I'm bizarrely awake.

"I need to take care of things," I say, out loud, but to myself.

Antoine nods while quietly eating his Acai. I'm not sure it's even possible for him to know what I'm talking about. The sun starts setting between the large mountains on the horizon, and, without talking, we start making back toward Ipanema.

Chapter 19

Stretched out on my bed at the *Casa*, paralyzed by lactic acid and my face stinging all over, I crack open my laptop. I'm surprised to find how easy it is to book an early return flight, and I do, in earnest.

The heavy tropical rain outside has me feeling better for not staying here any longer, while my online life confirms the earth is still spinning on its axis: Selena assures me she is "over" everything I "did" to her. Mandy put up an instructional video in a spandex bikini, giving new and exciting connotations to the downward dog position. My mom has escalated the panic level to Orange on the Homeland Security scale. And Hal is *OMG! Getting married soon! Dying to party it up like a free man in mtl FOR-THE-LAST-TIME!!*

I log on to Gmail, and quickly find Andy lurking.

Andy: *Charles? Window closing fast ...*
Charles: *Window?*
Andy: *PL enforcing their buy-out in court*

Charles: *So be it.*
Andy: ??? *all this for nothing?*
Charles: *what do you propose?*
Andy: *we accept Warner deal, negotiate a release sum from PlayLouder in return for agreeing not to target their existing database of artists ... best of both worlds.*
Charles: *and that means what for me?*
Andy: *u start Warner life in NY in 2 weeks ... don't know if I can even sell this, but if I can, we should jump through hoops.*
Charles: *I feel like a circus animal already*
Andy: *Is that a yes?*

I close the window and click back toward Mini's site, then my inboxes. Nothing for going on fourteen days now. Practice detachment, I keep telling myself. That great cure against the agony of hope. The sting from the disappointment is almost gone.

I hear a knock on my door and it opens at the same time.

"Hi Charles!" Françoise says.

"Hey there." I say.

"So I heard you were a big star on the beach yesterday?" she asks, gleaming with friendliness. I look away. "Come have a drink with us downstairs!"

"Thanks, but I'm good. Actually headed home in a couple of days, so need to start preparing stuff."

"What? So you *have* to come! There's a couple of new people that came in also. Come!"

I relent, painfully get up, and we walk downstairs together.

The group is sitting on the sofas and converged around a guy I don't recognize, as Françoise and I walk into the living room.

"So the copper's just standing there, *right* in front of me," the guy says, crossing his fingers, his large hands culminating in carved-out knuckles that seem just about ready to burst out of the skin. "Just staring. He's not moving, I'm not moving. I'm basically a cornered rat. This would be my third offense in a year. Now, this is the U.K., right? But we do three strikes you're out just like the Yanks do. Getting arrested's just *not* going to happen. Not with all the publicity my last expo got. Some fuckin' mid-aged twat bureaucrat would slap me on the poster of some new bollocks campaign for urban security. Anyway, my days as anonymous street artist would be done. Guaranteed."

He pauses, takes a long draw of his cigarette. His cavernous eye sockets punctuate a large, shaved skull. He's all shadows and bones; somewhere between a night-crawling hacker and a battle-tested hooligan. Yet his speech is slow and purposeful, his voice bizarrely engaging.

"Then," he continues, "don't know what's going on in my fuckin' head, swear, I grab my can of black spray-paint and PSSSHHHHT, just spray the fucker right in the face!! The copper starts yellin', reaches for his holster, but I'm off, zig zaggin', cuttin' through alleys, jumpin' fences. My occupation dictates I *always* carry a change of clothes in my bag. So barely a minute later, I'm good as new. Head to toe. I'm gone, disappeared. Been doing this since I'm eleven. But swear, never felt the fear of God himself until right then."

Everyone's staring at him wide-eyed, except for Chela, who's tending to his thoughts pensively across the room. Françoise and I find a spot on one of the couches.

"Dion," he stretches a hand in our direction, then fills two coffee mugs with carton wine and hands them to us, knocking his cup on ours.

"So, what happened?" one of the Irish girls asks him.

"Well, basically, here I am!" he stretches out. "But that was the last pinch for me. What with all my runnin' mates having cashed in, I was doin' the same old tricks, but with a crew of sixteen year olds now."

"What do you mean?" the Irish girl asks. "I mean, what kind of same old tricks?"

"Just stenciling the city with the randomly perverse and subversive. You know, policewomen making out, fighter jets droppin' gifts on war zones, that sort of thing. We were completely anonymous for years, just raidin' for fun. Then this guy from Sotheby's gets in touch with one of my mates, convinces him to put together a one off exhibit. They reckon street art's the next big *art movement* or whatever. And, just like that, we go from outlaws to celebs, matter of weeks. Fuckin' half the Hollywood jetset makes it out for the flashin' cameras. Brangelina, Johnessa, Posh and Becks, the rest of the two-headed media monsters. Out to bleed somethin' authentic into their personal brands. Anyway, there's four main guys in my crew, we each walk out with over a million quid. Mine's the largest – three mil'. And here it fuckin' goes."

"Hell of a success story," I say, surprising myself for even saying anything.

"Like hell is right," he answers. "Success like a fame transmitted disease. Now it's pop art and posters, Dion prints up for sale to tweenage girls and bobo yuppies. I heard even cops are crackin' walls now, to take pieces of my stuff down and sell'em. Last I heard I was being called to court back home. Some building owner suing the city for taking one of my prints from his wall. Estimates his losses in the six digits. When you're worth that much, they don't even *allow* you to be fuckin' illegal." Introspective now, he says, "That may have played a part in me sprayin' that copper, thinking of it now ..."

Everyone stays quiet for an instant.

"But anyway," he continues, "it happened, and I hit the airport the next day. To Rio!" He raises his voice, stands up and knocks his cup on whoever raises theirs. "To all the beautiful madness and chaos and pleasure of it!"

Chela and Antoine stare at each other with a look I immediately recognize as "intelligently sceptical."

"I'm sorry," Chela says, eyes now converging on him, "but you know, unfortunately, this is not a paradise. People have all the crazy fun so they can escape. But the violence is very real."

"Small price to pay for a bit of spontaneity, don't you reckon?" Dion answers with an amused, mischievous grin.

The Irish girls and Françoise stare at each other, unsure, then chuckle silently.

"No, but seriously, Chela is right," Antoine says, thinking man face on. "There's a big social dislocation issue here. And the unemployment is killing...."

"Unemployment?" Dion exclaims, almost in disbelief. "You mean humans actually not jailed up in square boxes? Perish the fuckin' thought!"

"Funny," Chela tries to butt in, "but...."

"... a little blood here," Dion ignores Chela and cackles as he knocks cups with his coalition of the willing once more, "a little corporal freedom there, sounds like nature on a good, healthy day to me!"

He notices me smiling, which I do out of amusement for his breaking the tediousness of these discussions more than out-and-out agreement with what he's saying.

"Ask this bloke here," Dion says, pointing to a still healing laceration on my forehead. "He looks to know a raucous ol' time in nature from a dreary couch conversation!" Chela looks him on, eyes almost glazed over.

"It may sound funny like this, now," Chela says, in a tone slightly more subdued than usual this time, "but you say *nature* like it's something to be taken advantage of."

Smiles turn to silent, awkward gazes.

"We already take *way* too much advantage of it already," Chela continues. "I think we need to control our desires if we want to stop destroying it. Otherwise, we're just killing ourselves in the long run."

"And a good thing that would be, wouldn't it?" Dion says with a snarky laugh, getting more animated. "The Earth may be choosing to flush us out, and I figure it'd be just about time, don't you reckon? And you see us as saviours? I mean, c'mon! The planet's got a few billion years either way of mankind's existence on it. In the long run, we're nothing but a small, self-conscious blip in the history of it! We don't have the *power* to destroy nature, much less save it! Nature *mocks* your pity! It *mocks* your benevolent intentions! That arrogant humanitarian junk! Environmentalism is just man's vanity turned virtuous. Nature's beyond good, evil, life, death, everything! We can accept its gifts with humility, or sit on arse and pretend it *depends* on us. Conceits of the mediocre human mind! Like right now, right this second," he gets up and starts making toward the door. "me, you, *us*, everyone in here," he points around, "we can choose to listen to the lullabies of each other's voices, or we can get up, get out, and go receive some of that planetary fruit!"

"But don't you think," Chela asks, before Dion's proposal can garner much momentum with the others, "that if we were less attached to the illusory goal of our own glory, we could live in better harmony with our surrounding?"

"I think that kind of western Buddhism's a legal anti-depressant, for starters," Dion answers. "Like the real you isn't the *you* that works in a soulless bureaucracy ten hours a day, but the person in Pilates class on Tuesdays, or laid out on a couch grandstanding while the world keeps changing out there, constantly. No wonder resignation echoes so well with us *Westerners* nowadays! It allows us to be as small and mediocre and private and cowardly as we secretly want to be! It's a narcotic, a pacifier of the first order! The executive class would be thrilled that we should be unthinking machines by day and self-abnegating wannabe monks hooked on entertainment by night."

"So what are you saying?" I cut in, figuring the last few days have given me my share of "inapplicable life theories" for at least a lifetime. The others stare at me, surprised that I've broken my usual silence. "What is it that you're proposing?" I demand, seeking to put Dion on the spot.

"Well I refuse to be spoon-fed, to start," he snaps back, as though he's had this conversation endless times before, "and, by that token, I also refuse to spoon feed others. But since you ask, I think the fetish of personal enlightenment is as corrosively individualistic and sterilizing as that of material success. It's another self-centered maze that leads to the same illusions of self-importance. I say if your heart is limited to your own comfort and self-preservation, you're barely warm dead meat already. In the long lens of big history, you're already a corpse. Like now, *right now*, I," he gets up, "am actually gonna stop *my* talking sounds and take any of you who want to follow into an example of what that can be ..."

"But no, you see, that's also what I mean," Chela interrupts. "I'm in Rio for two years now, but I don't *need* to go crazy like the Carnaval people on television! It's not a circus!" Antoine nods silently in approval.

"Haven't you guys ever considered," I say, "that maybe this guy has a point? I mean, maybe this is all just meaningless babble? We're here, talking monkeys in outer space, making all these elaborate sounds. But nothing we say *really* changes much of anything. We like to think we're these great big beings. But at the end of the day, we just do whatever's best for ourselves, and then we croak, and then that's the end of it, isn't it?"

"What I'm *not* talking about is that bullshit urban cynicism," Dion says, pensively drawing on his smoke. "That just makes you as passive and resigned and disconnected from anything other than your limited ends as the rest of the enlightenment crap."

"Hey man, who do you think you are?" Chela says.

The others slip into a sudden awkward silence, and Dion looks at Chela with a menacing stare.

"You don't even know this guy!" Chela says, recoiling back a little.

"And I am now *done* in here," Dion says, and starts to walk toward the door. "Anyone coming with?"

"Me!" The Irish girl who brought Dion in says.

"Me, too!" Françoise says. "Antoine, tu viens?"

"Non, ça va. You guys go ahead." Antoine answers.

"Charles?" Françoise pleads.

"No, I'm staying in too." I answer. "Have to get stuff ready for...."

And then, I look at them, Chela and Antoine, moribund, cerebral, on one side, and Dion and the girls on the other.

"You know what?" I mutter to myself and get up. "Sure, let's go."

Dion sets us on a brisk walking pace right as we step out of the *Casa*'s rusty gate.

"We headed anywhere specific?" I ask him, the girls just a couple of steps behind us, chatting casually.

"Naaah," Dion mutters lowly. "Just outta there. One more minute and I'd'a ripped someone's face off. Probably my own, too." His eyes are brimming enigmatically.

I tap my screen to a new e-mail from Nick.

"Okay, I'm just gonna...." He grabs my iPhone, and pitches it high, farther than I can follow.

"What the fuck!!" I yell and give him a punch-shove; but he doesn't react with the aggression I anticipate.

"Calm down, will you," he says, barely breaking a step. "Just keep walking. Trust me."

"Hey, *fuck you* keep on walking!" I yell out. "And no, I *don't* trust you! You just destroyed my phone, you goddamn prick!"

"Just keep low," he says, voice getting quieter, pace faster. The girls are now a good ten steps behind. "Last thing we need is to give these kids another reason to dice us up. That thing screams rich arse out here. Besides, it'll get you killed indirectly, too. Cancer. Balls and brain." He points to the two places simultaneously, and starts laughing a crazy laugh. "Got to fuckin' love this place, don't you? It does exactly what nature does, only amplified!"

I stop us and take hold of his arm.

"Okay, that's it!" I burst out, sick of his antics, and, in so doing, realize how much pent up frustration he'd already generated in me. "Who do you think you are? And where the hell are you taking us?" I wait for a second, but he doesn't answer. His eyes are now low and quiet, like a murderer's.

"I still can't believe you did that," I continue, as the girls catch up to us. "Dude, in the real world I'd have...."

"Would have *what*?" he says firmly, rising to meet my stare, but revealing no emotion. "*Fired* me? *Denounced* me?"

I'm not sure what to respond. The girls are listening now, concerned and quiet.

"Okay, I'll tell you what Mr. Charles," he says. "Basically, tonight's a pretty historic mission for me."

"What? What do you mean, a *mission*?"

"Unveiling a new stencil I'm quite proud of, in fact," he says and pats his backpack. "Look, I'm not gonna waste good time explaining. That's for the monks and schoolboys back there. But this one's an epic for me, and I thought it'd be something to have a few people to share it with." He points to the three of us. "If you do come, though, you have to trust, and follow, and listen the first time. Seize it now, or go back to playin' make-believe with the others."

His tone is in no way aggressive or insistent, just that of someone who requires a straight answer, and fast. His stare is piercing and I now realize he has no eyebrows at all, in fact, no hair anywhere; his head is like a massive helmet, his ears long and sharp. He's a goblin, I'm thinking, straight out of the underworld. And yet, I feel no fear. For some reason, I decide to nod. "Okay," I say, feeling a brief burst of exhilaration, "you know what, I'm in. Let's do this."

"Umm, guys?" Françoise says. "I think we're going to go back, okay?" she says, giggling and acting slightly freaked out. "Good luck though!" And both of them turn around and start walking back in the opposite direction.

"So, let's go," Dion says, and starts light jogging.

Ten minutes in, I'm impossibly fatigued and sweating profusely as we slip through one cobbled alleyway after another. I realize I'm completely lost and dependent now – I couldn't get back to the *Casa* if I wanted to. We take a couple of turns, and the streets gets narrower, the human chatter more and more distant.

"Here," He whispers, leading me through a rusty, waist-high fence.

"Where are we?" I ask, wondering where my judgement vanished just as it may have been most needed. All I see is a constricted stairway of broken stones snaking upward, and a slew of satellite dishes littering the sky like a fleet of UFOs. My sense of smell is saturated by a stench clocking in somewhere between rotten bananas and drenched, aging wood.

"Just shush and follow," he whispers hoarsely in my ear. Whatever's left of my intuition sends me signals to find an immediate escape.

"You're here now," he says, as though reading my thoughts. "Just come!"

He leads us swiftly up a half-dozen steps, and suddenly takes a hard left. I'm having difficulty following; he's like a sleek shadow, knifing through the air with purpose, and it's so dark I'm reduced to using sound as much as possible. I try to suppress the noise of my heavy puffing, and feel grateful for that soccer match having at least somewhat kick-started my lungs before this. Sidestepping a few scattered obstacles, he stops us beside what seems to be a deserted outdoor basketball court with a large, concrete wall behind it.

"Quick," he says.

He opens his small backpack, and reveals a large folded up piece of cardboard and four spray cans.

"Here," he points to the cans. "Black, white, blue and red. Keep this." He shoves the bag into my chest.

For the first time, I sense something resembling nervousness in him; his movements are not as perfectly controlled anymore, his whispering shakier.

"I say the color, you pass the can, then put the previous one back in the bag. Stay on the lookout. If anyone pops up, you tap my left shoulder twice. No words, nothing. We get up and speed walk back down as fast as we can. No questions. We're out of here seven minutes tops."

He takes out a piece of cardboard and scotches its edges to the wall.

"Black."

I hand over the can. The irregular hiss of the spraying can makes it a definable human sound in the silent darkness, and only contributes to my mounting nervousness.

"White."

And so on, until we've been there for at least fifteen long, drawn out minutes.

Then, as I'm still on a petrified lookout for on-comers, he finally says, "Done!"

I turn to the wall, but can't make out anything he's done in the dark. I instinctively start walking to leave.

"Wait up," he says, and takes out a small camera. "Only proof this ever happened!"

He measures up and snaps a few times. The flash bounces off the wall and briefly illuminates a mounting hill of dilapidated shacks behind him.

"Show me!" I whisper, and as he gets closer to me, we hear steps.

"Que é?" A voice says, coming from above us, shattering whatever fragile excitement had mounted in me.

Dion turns his head and motions for me to relax with one hand. We hear a couple of hoarse dog barks.

"Que é?" The voice insists, getting closer now.

The steps are coming faster and in our direction now. Dion taps my shoulder and says, "Okay, go!"

He takes off, me right on his heels, as we both jump the fence and race down the street.

"So?" Dion places the camera in front of my face as soon as we enter the gates of the *Casa*. I take a look but don't answer right away as I'm still pulling for air.

A policeman with a large smile bent over, handing over what looks to be a bouquet of flowers to two small black children. Only in place of roses and blooms are machine guns and grenades.

"No stylization on reality there, Charlie," he says, also catching his breath. "This is straight what's going on. Corrupt coppers selling guns to dispossessed and drugged up little buggers, who then turn and use those same guns on each other."

"I can't believe you made us do that!" I say. "You realize we could've easily died?"

"Well, then, at least we'd've been part of a damn decent story, wouldn't we?"

"You're fucking nuts. And my phone!"

"Couldn't take the risk of that thing ringing out there, or even vibrating," he points to the snapshot, "I'm sure you appreciate that now."

I throw my hands up in despair and decide to make for my room.

"You in for another?" he asks behind a devilish grin.

"Another?" I say. "Another *what*?"

"Well, that was just round one for tonight!"

"You must absolutely be fucking joking!" I say.

"Nope. Banging out another. It'll be easier though – we hit Leblon, the rich neighborhood this time. Got a great one of a nice white couple looking like vamps. And no favela gangsters to deal with. Although with those Brazilian coppers...." he says, thinking this through, as though making an elaborate calculation. "Not really sure we'd be that much safer than at the favela. Anyway, that would officially make it an epic run! Rozinha and Leblon in one night!"

"Epic? Are you serious? You'd actually risk getting us killed again just to be *epic*?" I demand, outraged. "Didn't you get enough of your fifteen minutes' worth of fame at that last expo of yours?"

He turns his head and locks my eyes, face dead serious all of a sudden. "And, in your learned estimation, fame is the only possible motivation I could possibly have for all this, is it?"

"I guess …" I start, not really having thought it through. "I mean, what else?"

"And gifts of the best you have to give of yourself, for the sake of something *other* than yourself, that doesn't count for much in your calculation, does it?"

"Please," I snicker. "You don't know me in real life. But I've worked alongside supposedly idealistic artists for years. And let me tell you, they're just as vain and selfish as the rest of us. I've had a front row seat to that show."

"Oh, really," he says, in a mocking tone, "and in what capacity have you worked with these artists?"

"Helped them out like crazy, for the most part," I say. "Basically invented a whole system for them to be discovered in a completely new, powerful way."

"And your own success and recognition were just a convenient by-product of all that, I presume?"

"Hey, at least I've always been honest about it," I say, as he forces me to smile, remembering all the exciting times PlayLouder provided me. "I never pretended to be doing it …"

He looks at me skeptically.

"Well, we all need to do *something* for a living, right?" I say. "At least I created my own form of meaningful work. I wasn't a slave like the others, at least for some time. But I lost it. Every bit of it. Been grasping at straws ever since. If that makes you feel any better."

"I read a little fable about work one day, when I was a kid," he says slowly, ignoring my remark, "spray-painted on a trash bin in south London, and I think it changed my life."

I pause, not sure whether to take him seriously.

"Once upon a time," he starts, "in the woods, there were a bear and a bee, and they were the best of friends. All summer long the bee worked hard to collect nectar from the flowers, morning to night. Meanwhile the bear was laying on his back, relaxing by the lake, basking in the long grass."

All of a sudden, Dion's calm, his eyes focused. His voice is stable and serious again. "When winter came, the bear realized he hadn't worked all summer, and so he had nothing to eat. He sat there and thought to himself, man, I really hope that my busy bee friend will share some of his honey with me. So he started looking for his friend. But the bee was nowhere to be found," Dion pauses. "Because the bee had died of a stress-induced coronary heart disease."

"Not bad," I say, as I can't help but let out a genuine chuckle. "But unfortunately, working too hard's not the issue for me at the moment. It's not working at all."

"Or maybe it's in fooling yourself to pretend there must be some massive significance in something that, at the end of it, you seem resigned to be doing strictly for self-driven reasons."

"Well, there's certainly no chance of me becoming some pseudo-enlightened guru wannabe like Chela, if that's where you're going."

"Hey, enlightenment, entertainment, enlight*ainment*, work, it's all basically the same mechanism, to me. Whatever sacrifices the weight of freedom for the lightness of ego. No matter how lofty the goal, it's an enslavement to personal needs in a society that manufactures them like essential fuel. Gurus and bosses are as needy as their cult members and slave-employees."

"Interesting theory," I say. "Unfortunately, none of it helps me figure out what I really want out of life at the moment."

"What you *really want*? That's really the limit of it for you, isn't it? There isn't any deeper question you can possibly manage to ask yourself, is there? What secret corner of my soul hasn't been showered with sushi and tits and champagne bubbles yet! Just like it never occurs to you that I'm willing to risk getting killed for a reason other than personal glory. Have you ever considered that if things and people have importance only insofar as they provide you with enjoyment, then they're all doomed to be ultimately futile in the face of your own inevitable death? That's the real face of your supposedly *sophisticated* cynicism. You're too needy to ever let things be themselves. And the world will never reciprocate the enormous importance you give yourself. You're the eternal victim of your own cosmic clumsiness."

"First of all what I was doing *was* pretty important ..." I hesitate, confused. "And anyway, what does that even mean? Anything anyone ever does is for a personal reason, at the root of it. Pretending otherwise is fake and hypocritical. There's no point."

"The point," he says, looking away and into his thoughts now, "is to stop being a slave to the confines of your own person. To taste action and thought divorced from the cravings of your umbilical self. To experience true freedom on earth. The point is royalty. Living like fucking royalty of the mind."

"Right! Royalty!" I say, getting up, realizing I'm just about done with this conversation. "Trust me, that's last thing on earth I feel like!"

"You ever consider," he says, smirking with a sly smile, "that maybe that's part of your problem?"

Chapter 20

Breakfast draws a full crowd at the *Casa*. I've Googled Dion and found every effusive epithet, good and bad, attached to his name in the U.K. press. But it's hard to separate reality from myth, the average opinion of him falling somewhere between "street Picasso" and "punk degenerate."

Dion storms in and quickly downs a banana.

"Mornin', everyone!"

Chela is chatting silently to a group of three, giving Dion a cold shoulder he doesn't notice.

A few seconds later, Françoise walks in, in a tight see-through tank top, purple pajama pants and some of the best humor I've ever seen her in.

Dion caresses her waist, a gesture that would have easily passed unnoticed, but is somehow magnified as everyone's eyes are glued to him. I turn and smile to Antoine with compassion.

"Whatever. It's okay." Antoine whispers to me. "You know it's not like that with me and her."

Shortly after breakfast, everyone is off, and Dion intercepts me just I start making for my room.

"Not joining Gilligan's crew?" he asks me.

"Packing today, actually," I answer, avoiding him.

"Want to join for a jog?"

"Don't think so," I say, and get up. But I'm unable to contain my curiosity. "So, did you end up doing the Leblon thing last night?" I ask.

"Sure did!" he says. "And I learned a valuable lesson. To run away from the law, you need one thing above all others." He pauses. "Good cardio! Come on now!"

I relent and we speed walk out of the gates, which gives me a disturbing déjà vu of last night. I do my best to keep up as we run across Ipanema Beach, up to the mid-way point of Copacabana beach. By then, I've forced us to slow down to a lead-footed walking pace.

"Alright, forget this," Dion says. "Pretty obvious you're not running away from anything with legs anytime soon."

"Yeah," I puff out.

"Yeah, whatever. Here," he points to an open beach bar where we notice a few people jamming with small instruments. "This more your bag?"

"Yes!"

"Drinks, then?" he asks, and starts walking toward the bar.

I gather myself. "Sure. Just not long. Still have to pack."

We sit at one of the small tables and start ordering in succession. I've regained some of my composure and the slow, steady instrumentals are calming me. But I'm having difficulty focussing, with the sun getting more intense, splashing down on us and reflecting off the water and tables and glasses. The cuts on my face are in a constant tingle. Dion is teeing off at a devil's debit, and I've given up trying to follow him fully.

"Look at 'em, below the poverty line and serving up quadruple shots for the price of one. So we got poor givers and rich beggars in this world...."

Nod.

"Religion isn't man's description of how he believes the world really works. It's the pact he makes with his fears...."

More nods.

I rub sweat off my face every few seconds. My gaze is suddenly drawn toward to the statue of Christ perched atop the Corcovado. How different it is from the cross I've been watching atop the Mount Royal, every day from my office window the last six years! Jesus here is a live man, donning a long toga, arms stretched out, almost in admiration of the spectacle before him. The victim makes way to the sensualist, the judge of man seems more like his adoring fan. In Montreal, it's only the cross – no man. The whole world is little more than the theater of his suffering.

I wipe more large beads of sweat out of my eyes, and my stare shifts to the musicians.

"Wait," I tell Dion, and I head toward them.

They're talking calmly between songs; I circle them a couple of times. My eyes confirm what I thought they had perceived at first, but I go around them a third time to make sure. Finally, I walk over, as though clasping toward a mirage. I take a deep breath, acting as casual as I can fake.

"Mini?" I say.

"Hey...." she hesitates, "hi there!"

Her not mentioning my first name gives me a sinking feeling. She looks different – her browner skin tone makes her tattoos seem less harsh, and her hair is an even lighter shade of blond. She gets up from her group and we walk slowly together toward the corner of the bar. She gives me a friendly push on the arm. "I can't believe you are here!"

"Yeah, I know, me, too," I say, working to sharpen up. "I told you, I was ... into living more spontaneously, I...."

"Great!"

Her positive energy is overflowing, but I don't get the sense that it's necessarily directed toward me.

"Yeah, I actually sent you an e-mail," I say. "Wasn't sure if you'd made it out here or if you were just talking."

"Ha!" she yelps. "I came a few days after. But I don't check e-mails here!" She looks around. "I mean, a screen can't compete with this, you know?"

"Yeah, tell me about it," I say, thinking back to my endless hours at *Lettras*. "Totally agree with you."

"So how long have you been here?"

"Just a few days. But it ... feels like longer, you know?"

"Yeah, it does that," she says with a friendly wink as she gestures to one of her friends. Looking at her move and talk, I'm slowly reconfirming to myself the reason I came here.

"So are you staying for a while?" she asks.

"Actually, today's my last day. My plane is leaving tonight. Yeah, just some important stuff I still needed to take care of back home, you know?"

"Well, that's too bad," she puts her hand on my forearm. "Listen, I have to get back to my friends. But what time are you leaving?"

"I don't know. Seven?" I say, then reconsider. "Maybe seven thirty?" The latter of which would leave me roughly an hour to reach the airport and catch an international flight.

"Ahh, that's too bad," she says. "Some of us are checking out the sunset here together around eight. I would have told you to come."

"You know what?" I answer. "I think I could maybe manage that."

Chapter 21

I get out of the cab, walk down to the Copacabana beach post. I take off my shoes and walk on the warm sand for a few minutes before I spot a group sitting by the beachfront. My flesh is still throbbing at different spots – burnt shoulders and nose, moist slashes and bruises on my face and hands. But a warm, merciful breeze is blowing on me. Mini and I lock eyes almost immediately as I approach her group. She motions for me to join them.

"Hi, everyone," I say, unable to suppress frustration at all the wait and indecision she's generated in me. "Mini, can we talk for a minute?"

"Ya, sure," she gets up casually, and we walk a few steps away from the others.

"So ... what's up?" I ask, feeling an urge to connect with her. "I'm leaving here in an hour. Just tell me. What's up between us?"

"What do you mean *what's up*?" she asks, simply.

If I had any doubts as to what I found in her, as to whether she was worth the efforts I'd made, they're dissolving now under the fading sun. Large, diamond-shaped blue eyes, perfect, plump breasts filling her green bikini. She looks like Eve herself might've had she been an underground Berliner. "We're just enjoying, no?"

I decide that sometimes fate needs help, and take hold of her hand. I pull her gently toward me and grab her waist. But she resists and gently pushes back.

"Charles?" she says, her usual state of nonchalant bliss broken for the first time.

"Okay, so all this for what, exactly?"

"All *this*?"

"I mean, to have a guy meet you halfway across the world. And then act like...." I look at her, and she seems back in a state of peace, sporting only a look of mild concern now, which only accentuates my grief and confusion. "I don't know," I throw up my hands. "Honestly. I just don't know."

"I understand now, Charles. But I don't think *you* understand *me*." She rests her hand on my shoulder. The skin contact brings my emotions down a notch. "I'm here with someone. My long-time partner, actually."

She turns to the group and points toward a slender, dark-skinned brunette.

"No," I say, stumbling. "No way! That is a lie."

"No, really!" she answers, keeping my stare with a look of amazement. "We're together two and a half years!"

I drop my suitcase to the sand. An unfamiliar emotion enters me from the head on down, like a penetrating probe. I take a quick glance at Mini, conscious, now, of the pathetic pride that had welled up in me for having brought myself to follow her, big spontaneous proud push of the illusory mind, utterly blind to the fact that she never was, in fact, *could never have been*, interested in the way I'd hoped or imagined. An impossible romance to match an impossibly self-fabricated reality.

"I'm sorry," she says. "I thought...."

I let go and walk a few steps away, lifting my head upward. It feels as though a thin veil were lifted from in front of me, allowing me to experience, viscerally, just how self-absorbed I'd become, unable to discern outside reality from the running internal commentary that plagues me. I turn my head and observe the objects and people around. Is it possible that the purpose of all this goes beyond my personal consumption of it, as object of understanding, growth opportunity, meaning generation, escape valve, pleasure instrument, theatre of self-realization? The mountains stand guard on the horizon as the favelas spill down from them like a massive trail of debris, the waves crashing softly around the Corcovado, the tropical flora growing on top of the broken-down shacks. All of it just *there*, inchoate, irregular, co-existing effortlessly, one thing giving to the other and receiving from the next in a great unconscious dance. My mind fails to grasp the intricate relationships between them, but I realize its impotence doesn't affect any of it in the slightest. Time seems to stop for an instant, the elements around me appear to hang in suspense for a brief moment, infused, it seems, with a new density, a new *weight* about them.

Is my idea of "personal freedom" anything other than a Sisyphean burden to satisfy whatever cravings happen to grip my mind? Is it possible that my endless cycle of needs is not a compass pointing toward my liberation, but is the very thing preventing it from ever really happening? That my "*what I really want*" mantra is little more than a fetish for meaning, a vapid narcissism, the selfish impulse abstracted into a spiritual signpost? Through the lens of my infinite desire to receive reality for myself alone, I now sense that, just like I've done with Mini, I could never allow people and things be *really* themselves. I'd simply dismembered them into segregated collections of attributes, to be reconstituted along the constellations of my personal whims. In fact, the whole world had become little more than my personal instrument – to be used, at times, for elation, at other times for contempt and victimization. *Always*, however, used in a linear march of bloated self-importance. Is a Copernican revolution of the *self* even conceivable?

The hypothesis alone makes me dizzy. And yet, there's no joy as I think of this, not even through a kind of meaningful pain I can take pride in. I simply feel *small*. And finally! What a relief, not having to bear the weight of the entire universe by ceasing, even for a brief instant, to be its sole and final destination. For the first time, I perceive my whole being as a particle in a surrounding organism, part of an eternal spectacle it is not, and will never be the endpoint of. How has my labyrinthine, over-stimulated, self-aggrandizing mind sanctioned me as the culmination of something so exponentially greater than myself?

All my perceived authenticity – zealous opposition to all establishments, my utopian crusade for artistic independence, my pain-fueled judgments of all those surrounding me – was any of it really much more than a private collection of flags and badges, elaborate self-spun storylines plotting nothing but my own personal legend? Or had I simply become a serial collector of emotional wounds and victories, a champion grudge-holder and medal-bearer, a wizard at converting real and imagined slights into a dizzying narcotic of ambition and pain? After all, there is also great importance in being a great victim. In a self-scripted fall from grace, I'd simply exchanged the object of my narcissism: from accomplishment to desecration, from being admired by others to being used by them, never ceasing, even for an instant, to be the object of their fascinated attention. I had condemned myself to absolute relevance. It's all too suspect to live on. My sense of self, erected into a science, an art, a psychology, a religion, a God, all in one, a deformed matrix of self-affirming meaning, has grown disgustingly, horrendously suspect.

Then, as suddenly as things seemed to stop around me, they start again, but moving to a slower rhythm this time, less random, more deliberate, dissolving what feels like years of mental constructs under a quickly fading light. The sun drops another degree down the horizon, its waning movements making the shadows from the trees and plants appear suddenly large and dominating.

Mini is standing a few steps away from me, the others are still a few meters beyond us.

"The best show on earth," she says, her girlfriend next to her. I'm not sure I understand, but refrain from saying anything. Instead, I turn back toward the shifting colors of the skyline and allow the low, humming intensity of an intentional quietness take me over.

And then, just as the bottom of the enlarged, crimson sun begins sinking below the distant ocean-line, she, along with everyone else around us, erupts into a cheerful applause.

Three days of simplified bliss to my physical self now pop up onscreen as three months' worth of hell to my digital alter ego.

I'm at *Lettras*, skimming through dozens of unread e-mails, seasoned by generous punctuation marks, their tentacles reaching for the back of my brain. I scour the titles quickly. Sandwiched between an alarmed mom and a quizzical Selena is an e-mail by Andy with the charming title "Game Over."

> *PlayLouder has filed an interim injunction against you for breach of contract. They're enforcing their buyout clause. Of course, all previous offers have been rescinded. Warner is also out of the picture. I can't continue representing you in these circumstances. You could at least call or write if you knew you weren't making it back when you said you would. Maybe you're dead, or worse. Something tells me you're not.*

Charles, you brought this on yourself. But you've ruined my rep with at least two of the majors. I can still make arrangements if you want to get back and figure out what's left of this mess. I'm pdf'ing you the motion materials. We can contest it in court next Wednesday.

Chapter 22

Andy shuffles the papers at his desk, eyes down, almost completely impervious to my presence.

"So you're saying it's over?" I ask.

He chuckles to himself.

"Well, I suppose it depends, Mr. Charles," he takes off his glasses, puts them on the table with a sombre face, still looking at the papers. "If by *it* you mean your career, your direction, your life, everything you've lived for the last six years, then yes, it is. *O-ver*. Between their all-star legal team and the main witness pulling a no-show, they won the motion handily. And made me look *really* bad. And got fees, too. Coming straight out of *your* buyout fee. And of course, there are my fees, on top of all that." He hands me a brown envelope. "Everything's in here."

I open it and briefly scan the words written in bold on the last page. DECLARE, ORDER, CONDEMN, COSTS.

"Warner's officially moved on, too," he says. "And after news broke out of Universal's direct involvement with PlayLouder, the company's been pretty much dismantled for its software."

"How do you know all this?"

"We live in a small town, Charles. Your friend Nick is back booking DJs for a living, and wants to know if I can help him somehow. Of course, I can't. And he told me Clarice got a job as a secretary at a real estate firm." He stares deep into my eyes with gravity. "You're the last man standing, Charles. No enemies, but despised by all your friends, as they say. Congratulations Mr. Barca."

"Strange time for sarcasm, Andy."

"Well, I'll be honest with you," he says. "I've never seen anything like this in my professional career. It's almost like you became so paranoid that you couldn't even bring yourself to act in your own basic self-interest."

He waits for an answer I don't give him.

"The *only* ray of light here," he continues, "is we still have three days to appeal this. And maybe – just maybe – it's not too late to put up a last ditch fight for Warner, maybe even to start you off in a lower role at first and work your way back...."

"We're not appealing," I say.

He looks up at me, puzzled. "Charles, you have the right to be depressed for losing your job, but...."

"I didn't lose my job, Andy. And I'm not depressed. In the least."

"You still have to pull yourself together professionally somehow," he says, ignoring me, "I mean, you do have this one year forced time-out now, but it's just twelve months. What are you going to do with your life after that?"

"Well, since you ask," I say, suddenly feeling excited to tell him. "I've decided to start a kind of free artist management Wiki." I take a sheet of paper and start drawing up a visual. "So, between star editors, vetted contributions from industry professionals and even the public at large, and some pretty basic artificial intelligence applications, we can loop and rate and groom information worldwide over time, and create this self-perfecting genie type application for any artist to use in their careers. For free! Basically, they could gain access to all the best contacts, advice and information in the world and not have to be locked in...."

"Free?"

"Yeah, for sure. Look, I realized PlayLouder was just using a new method to funnel artists into the same old hands. But a completely disinterested, de-centralized space like this could become the next great artistic hub. This is exactly what talent needs – unlocking the collaborative mind and mining it for the best advice, tailored to whatever situation they may be in."

"So you've destroyed the A&R career path," he says, coughing up a sarcastic laugh, "and now you're looking at managers as the next target to touch with that apocalyptic, black thumb of yours. Nice one! I'm sure that'll score you a whole bunch of new friends in the industry!"

"I was thinking more along the lines of liberating creators from the grips of another oppressive and parasitic business structure, to be honest."

"Yeah, look," he says, "I knew you before you became a virgin, right? You'll get tired of monkey-ing around after a couple of months. Not to mention you doing anything of that nature is probably against the judgement. But you still have three days to appeal this. That's your last chance, Charles, I'm telling you."

I pause and look into his eyes, two little black vortexes, leading straight into the void.

"Andy?" I say.

"Yes?"

"This may just be the last thing I ever end up telling you. You are NOT appealing."

And I walk out of his office.

I walk into my loft, close the door quietly behind me. I get on the Internet, and briefly consider online suicide by changing my passwords into random gibberish. Does a life never recorded online ever really occur at all? Instead, I glance at the un-listened to demo's stacked on top of my table, click to Facebook, cut and paste my internal notes about my new project and type: *Anyone in*?

I sit on the couch, close my eyes, open one of the demos, start listening. Average, big-city lonely chickoustic, built for play in nostalgic romcom's or the indie-pop movie cottage industry. I put in another. White trustafarian ska with folk undertones, a kind of poor man's child between Jack Johnson and Sublime with Frosh lyrics and a college radio DNA. Nothing special. But honest, communicative. Useful. I open my eyes and go back onscreen: thirteen "likes" already, more trickling in. E-mails start pouring in from various sources, industry and otherwise. There *is*, apparently, a market for selflessness. I open the brown folder, take out my judgement, start reading it carefully. It says I can't act for another online music project "as employee, employer, agent, joint-venturer, partner, shareholder, independent contractor, supplier, consultant or trustee." Doesn't say anything about *donor*. It *couldn't* be illegal to just help people for free, could it? Maybe the system can't stop what it can't conceive: a pure act of giving. Or maybe that is exactly what it has the most interest in eliminating. In an age ruled by ego, generosity may be the only revolutionary act left. Why do I get the feeling that the best intentions I can muster will end up shrouded in a new mess?

I look out the window. Old Montreal is much the same it's always been. Buzzing crowds, small merchants, government-financed construction crews humping the city dry. Nothing ever the final product of itself, everything locked in a long, tireless grind toward becoming something else, everyone and everything fuelled by a force both invisible and infinite.

The Saint Lawrence River is beaming reflections of a beauty that will never be into my loft, and my heart is full with the shifting strangeness of it all.

All is well, I'm thinking. All is well.

THE END

15271016R00117

Made in the USA
Charleston, SC
26 October 2012